LONGSHOT

Ten years ago, the Red Butte boys were one of the most powerful and deadly gangs in Arizona Territory, pulling off the Mountain Springs wagon robbery and netting $50,000 in gold certificates before disappearing. Since then, no sign of the gang or the loot has been seen, and it is assumed that the criminals are living off their ill-gotten gains in Mexico. But after one of the certificates surfaces in the town of Bisbee, maybe the robbers can be traced . . .

C. J. SOMMERS

LONGSHOT

Complete and Unabridged

LINFORD
Leicester

First published in Great Britain in 2014 by
Robert Hale Limited
London

First Linford Edition
published 2017
by arrangement with
Robert Hale
an imprint of The Crowood Press
Wiltshire

A catalogue record for this book is available
from the British Library.

ISBN 978–1–4448–3345–4

Published by
F. A. Thorpe (Publishing)
Anstey, Leicestershire

Set by Words & Graphics Ltd.
Anstey, Leicestershire
Printed and bound in Great Britain by
T. J. International Ltd., Padstow, Cornwall

This book is printed on acid-free paper

1

'It can't be done,' Laredo told Jake Royle flatly.

'You've done the difficult jobs before,' the pudgy man, who sat in stockinged feet behind the desk in the Territorial Bank Examiner's Office, said.

'This is not difficult, Jake,' Laredo answered. 'This is just plain — '

'Impossible,' Jake said, holding up a stubby hand. 'You're just being stubborn. It's that stubborn streak in you that I appreciate, Laredo. It keeps you going when other men give it up as being too difficult. Sure, I know it's a longshot . . . '

The tall man facing Jake Royle got to his feet, shrugged heavily and walked to the window, startling a mockingbird which had been perched on the window ledge. Laredo watched the bird wing away, scolding men and their ways.

'Tell me again,' Laredo said with his back still to Royle. 'Then I'll tell you again why it's impossible.'

'Very well,' Jake said, bending down to scratch his foot. The odor from his stockinged feet was not pleasant, but Laredo had given up mentioning it. When Jake had given up field work and taken the desk job in Flagstaff, he had sworn never again to wear his riding boots unless it was absolutely necessary. He said that he had tortured his feet enough in the twenty-some years he had spent chasing outlaws across Arizona Territory. Sighing with relief, Jake leaned back in his swivel chair and spoke to Laredo.

'I did mention that the loot taken was in gold certificates.'

'You did,' Laredo answered without apparent interest. 'And you said that it happened ten years ago, which makes the whole thing — '

'Ten years ago,' Royle went on, not waiting for the last word of Laredo's complaint, 'a transfer of funds was being made between the central bank and the branch in Tucson. Along the way, near a place called Mountain Springs, the wagon carrying the money got hit by a gang of robbers — six of them. They left most of the silver and small coins but made off with stacks of Series B gold certificates. About fifty thousand dollars' worth.'

'Which was probably all spent years ago. Likely all of the men who were involved are dead by now.'

'I want you to listen to me, Laredo — this time. Gold certificates don't just pop up everywhere like greenbacks. There aren't that many issued. In fact the Series B certificates were not issued again after the stick-up, and since these were brand new, crisp and stiff as boiled shirts, the printing office still had a list of the serial numbers, all sequential.'

'You told me that,' Laredo grumbled, crossing the room to return to his chair where he perched on the edge of the seat as if he had somewhere else he was supposed to be. If he was in a hurry, his boss was not.

'The best we could figure was that the robbers had probably made a beeline for the Mexican border. Down there at some exorbitant exchange rate they would have been able to sell the gold certificates to international dealers.'

'So the men you suspect are probably living well-fed, comfortable lives in their Mexican *casas*.'

'You would assume so; I have something to show you, though.' Jake opened his top desk drawer and removed an ornate bill, folded once exactly down the center. Laredo took it, examined it, noticing it was a Series B gold certificate in the amount of $500. Laredo had seen one only once before, and that was in a bank in Phoenix.

'Where'd it come from, Jake?'

'A horse trader named Randall Nye down in Bisbee accepted it as payment for a herd of horses he was selling. When he took it to the bank, they told him that it was stolen and they could not accept it. Then they confiscated it.'

'Must have made Nye mad.'

'Mad! They say he almost had a seizure in the bank lobby.'

'Well, you can't blame him,' Laredo commented.

'No,' Jake Royle agreed. 'But, you do see, Laredo, that means that at least one of the outlaws had come out of hiding long enough to purchase some horses.'

'And he probably drove them straight back across the border to Mexico.'

'Probably, but maybe not. They might have gotten into some trouble down there. You know all these men on the run have the idea of escaping to Mexico. But it's a different country: the language is different; the laws are different. It's a rough country, Laredo. Maybe one or some of the robbers have decided that things have quieted enough by now for them to come back to the States — after ten years.'

'That could be so,' Laredo allowed, 'but I can't see that this gets us any closer to finding them. You'd better tell me who you suspect. You were around back then; I wasn't.'

'Well, it's become pretty much common knowledge by now who some of them were. Men we suspected all along.' Jake took a cigar from his desk drawer, smelled it and placed it down. He liked a good cigar, but his doctor told him he was only smoking his way to an early grave and Jake had sworn to give them up.

'Who?' Laredo asked, interrupting Jake's longing for the cigar.

'Who? Well, there was a bunch of outlaws at that time called the Red Butte gang,' Jake replied. 'They sort of thinned out and drifted away about the time of the Mountain Springs hold-up. A few of them have never been seen since. Asa Taylor was the leader of the gang. I always thought he was involved in the stick-up. Then there was Winslow Pear and a man named Harry Speed — that's not the name he was born with; he had some kind of German name — although he was fast enough with a gun.'

'You have no proof, I take it.'

'No, except the money's gone, they're gone. Men around are saying that Asa was there for sure. You know how it is, Laredo, when something like this first happens, no one wants to be the one pointing fingers — afraid it will come back on them — so you can't pry a word out of anybody.

'After a while, men are willing to talk even if they don't really know anything, sort of basking in the reflected glory of the men who got away with the big heist.' Again Jake picked up the cigar, studied it with respect, and put it away.

'So what are you advising — that I talk to some of the old-timers around town?' Laredo asked.

'I never advise you on what to do, Laredo. You've always followed your own instincts and had a deal of success doing things your way. I only mentioned it as a possibility. One thing you will have to do is talk to this horse trader, Randall Nye, of course. He saw the man he was dealing with and will be able to give you some sort of description.'

'I've never seen any of these men you mentioned,' Laredo said, 'and after ten years, I don't know that I would recognize them even if I passed one on the street. Men change, and they're sure not going to give me their right names, if asked.'

'No,' Jake said, 'I know that. Do what you can, Laredo. Maybe you'll get lucky. I know this is the most difficult job I've ever given you, but fifty thousand's the biggest loss the bank ever had to swallow. I've said, I know it's a longshot, but if anyone can do it, it's you.'

'I'll give it a try,' Laredo said doubtfully. 'Of course I may not be back for ten years or so either.'

'You can draw cash from the Bank of Bisbee if you need it. I've already notified them.'

'Would you also write down the serial

numbers of the gold certificates? And, I'll need the names of the suspects you have and any kind of description you can give me.'

Laredo waited, looking out the window as Jake took care of that for him. As he watched a lumber wagon with six-feet-high wheels rolled past toward the sawmill on the opposite end of town. They were taking a lot of timber off the pine-clad slopes surrounding Flagstaff just now as if they feared they would run out of lumber before the building surge ended.

'Here you go,' Jake Royle said. 'Everything I can think of. You still might want to spend some time listening to the old-timers around town here. If you can sort out the bull from the truth, you might learn something.'

'All right, Jake,' Laredo said, tucking the sheet of paper away in his shirt pocket without glancing at it. There would be time enough to study it on the long ride to Bisbee. The two shook hands and Laredo left the office. By the time he had closed the door and stepped three strides down the corridor, he smelled the unmistakable scent of burning tobacco.

Outside it was cool, the sky clear except for a few wind-flagged high clouds floating like a bridal veil. Laredo made his way to the stable in search of the gray horse with the white-splashed chest he was riding these days. That horse would never win a race, but he was steady and easy to sit on the longest of rides.

Saddling up, he led the horse down the street toward the Destination Saloon, which Laredo knew had formerly been a hangout for some of the local badmen. It was not so much now. Most of the old-time outlaws had been gunned down, locked up or forced by age to retire from their former trade. Still, there were a few hanging around, cadging drinks in exchange for wild tales of the old days.

Tying up at the rail, Laredo went into the Destination and spotted his man immediately, sitting alone at the end of the bar, his hands folded on it, empty. Laredo edged through the collection of round card tables where dusty, whiskered men played loudly and cursed at intervals. Laredo went to the empty space at the end of the bar and positioned himself beside the little man with the slack jaw and angry expression, who barely glanced at him.

The small man's eyes were bloodshot, but also extremely yellow, Laredo figured that the man had done his time with the bottle and was now showing the signs of it. Ordinarily he would not have offered such a man a drink — but then it probably did not matter at this point in the deterioration of his health. Besides, whiskey was the common currency in situations, places like this. He spoke to the small man with the bitter eyes.

'How's the whiskey here, friend?'

'Scarce,' was the raspy reply.

'Well, then, can I stand you for one? I don't like drinking alone.' Laredo lifted a hand toward the chubby bartender, who was busy at the other end of the bar. The man at Laredo's elbow was studying him dubiously.

'I don't know you, do I?' he asked.

'No.' Laredo removed his arms from the bar so that the chubby man could serve them two whiskeys. 'Why?'

'I got a long habit of not drinking with lawmen,' the man said, although he picked up the glass and raised it to his lips with a trembling hand.

'So have I,' Laredo said with a grin, tilting his own glass. He was still being closely observed by his new-found drinking partner. 'The only reason I have a little silver in my jeans right now is I just got fired yesterday. The ranch boss and I had a little scuffle. I decided to fork my pony and ride until I found a friendlier situation. Of course it doesn't hurt to make a few stops along the way, kind of keep the spirits up.'

Laredo finished his whiskey — it was raw and had an unusual smoky aftertaste — and gestured for two more.

'Not much better than Indian whiskey, is it?'

'As long as it does the job without killing me,' the little man said. His hand was steadier this time as he gulped his second drink and stood back, trying to measure Laredo. 'Why'd you come up on me, stranger?'

Laredo grinned and choked his own second drink down. 'Someone,' he said, flagging his thumb across his shoulder in an indefinite direction, 'told me that you knew pretty much what was going on around here. That you might even be able to point me in a profitable direction.'

The man shook his head heavily and remained silent. Laredo motioned to the bartender again. His stomach was burning as the raw liquor settled there. One more of the job's penalties, he told himself.

'You mean you work with a gun,' the old-timer said, accepting a third drink. His red eyes seemed to be clearing up but retained their yellow cast.

'I didn't say that.'

'I understood your meaning,' the man said. 'I got to be honest with you: there was a time when I knew pretty much everyone who ran roughshod in this county, but now they're mostly gone, mostly dead, I suppose. Oh, a few made their big scores and got out of here, but mostly — '

'Like the old Red Butte gang?' Laredo asked innocently, signalling for more whiskey. The little man's eyes narrowed suspiciously.

'What do you know about them?' he asked in his cracked voice.

'Everybody knows about them and the Mountain Springs stage robbery,' Laredo said easily. 'Made them kinda famous.'

'Yeah . . . well, they're long gone now,' the drunk said, as if he had been briefly struggling with his conscience and the code of silence. 'Rich and comfortable somewhere, I suppose. I should have gone along with them that time . . . '

'I guess you knew them all,' Laredo nudged as the man drank his fourth whiskey. His tongue was well lubricated by now, apparently.

'Knew them all well enough,' the old man responded. 'Asa Taylor, Stoker, Harry Speed and the kid — what was his name?' His eyes went blank briefly and then brightened again. 'Les Hooper, that was it. He wanted to be as tough as Asa, as good with a gun as Speed, but he just didn't have it in him.'

'I don't suppose you knew Winslow Pear as well?' Laredo coached, remembering a name Jake had given him.

'Told you I knew them all, didn't I!' the man said with a hint of rising belligerence. He was getting close to the line as far as sobriety went. Laredo shrugged indifference. He now had the names of five of the gang responsible for the Mountain Springs robbery, for all the good it would do him. They were all likely 500 miles away from Flagstaff, alive or buried.

And they had, more than likely, run through the stolen money years ago.

Laredo left an extra silver dollar on the bar counter and went out into the brightly sunlit day. He remained in the shade of the canopy above the porch for long minutes, waiting for his eyes to adjust to the sunshine. He felt a little unsteady on his feet, having neither the taste nor inclination toward whiskey usually. The drinks had done little to the old man but bring him more fully alert. They seemed to have drained Laredo of his energy.

He felt more than heard the man in the black suit emerge from the saloon and stand behind him. A low voice muttered, 'I don't know what you're looking for, stranger, but you've found a sure way to take some bullets if you don't forget about Mountain Springs.'

The man walked hurriedly but calmly away. Laredo watched his back as he strode along the plankwalk. He thought it was someone he had seen sitting near him and the old man inside the Destination, but he was not sure. He had paid little attention to the man.

Apparently the man in black had paid some attention to Laredo and his conversation.

Laredo shrugged it off. No matter. He was leaving Flagstaff, riding far and there was no time for worrying about casual barroom threats, which were usually hollow. It made no difference; he could not allow it to make a difference. He had a job to do, and it was time he was getting to it.

2

Laredo rode southward slowly. There was a cool wind on his back and he had turned up the collar of his sheepskin coat. Ahead the empty land rolled away. He had passed a few outlying ranches after leaving Flagstaff, but now there was nothing built by man to be seen. It would be much warmer, drier after he reached the southern part of the state, but for now he managed to enjoy the cool mountain day, although it was not what you would call comfortable. The temperature was probably in the low 50s, and the breeze made it feel cooler.

The land no longer featured pine trees, and there was little game although he did startle a doe and her twin fawns in passing, saw an angry-looking badger which he gave wide berth. Now as he continued there were dozens of crows on the wing, circling, apparently going nowhere.

Bisbee. Laredo hadn't been down to Cochise County for a while; he couldn't imagine it had changed much. He knew the Cochise County Sheriff, Glen Radcliffe — assuming he still held the job. Not that long ago he and Radcliffe had had a misunderstanding about just who Laredo was and what his job entailed.

'Then you're some sort of bounty hunter,' Radcliffe had said, leaning back in his chair and grimacing as if the word left a bad taste in his mouth.

'No, sir, I am not.'

'But you're chasing the men who robbed the bank.'

'No, sir,' Laredo corrected, 'I am chasing the money that was taken from the bank. There is a difference. As I told you I work for the enforcement arm of the Territorial Bank Examiner's office. You, as sheriff, might be obligated to find the robbers. We — the banks and I — are only interested in seeing that the funds are recovered. I have no authority nor any desire to arrest those responsible. My job is strictly to find the misappropriated funds.'

'You don't try to arrest them?' Radcliffe had said, seated behind his desk in the county jail. 'So what do you do? Just ride up behind them and ask them kindly to give you the money back? It doesn't seem that many men would be likely to do that.'

'Not many,' Laredo said calmly, and the sheriff caught a glimpse of the determination in Laredo's eyes. 'That's when it's up to me to find a way to make them comply.'

Radcliffe thought that Laredo had forced more than a few men to comply. He said so.

'I didn't say that it was an easy job,' Laredo told him quietly.

But that was the point: Laredo did not pursue the men, but the money belonging to any bank in the Territory of Arizona. He wouldn't have cared if all the robbers went free so long as they returned the money. But as Radcliffe had commented, things seldom worked out that way.

He would have to talk to Radcliffe again on this trip, find out if he had heard anything, discover if he knew the character of the horse trader, Randall Nye. For it had occurred to Laredo that Nye might not have obtained the gold certificate in the manner he had described. There may have been no horses, no mysterious buyer. Nye could himself be one of the Red Butte gang come now out of hiding, and desperately trying to redeem one of the stolen bills.

There were many possibilities. Maybe Sheriff Radcliffe could tell him what he knew of the man. Laredo needed to interview Nye.

Laredo slept out that night and the night after. The land before him now began to flatten. It supported only the chaparral plants: mesquite, sage, manzanita, agave, and laurel-leaf sumac, although along the riverbeds sycamore, cottonwoods and willows grew along with scattered live-oak trees. He himself was hungry, not having wanted to waste a rifle cartridge on something so small as a jack rabbit which would likely have been blown to furry fragments by the rifle bullet, and not having time to fish the creek or set snares. Even though he had come across some larger game — the deer, for example — he did not want to pause long enough to dress out, butcher and cook venison. It was his choice not to, but still he was riding hungry.

He wondered how the man following him was faring.

Laredo could not be sure who it was, but he was positive that the man was back there, trailing him. The man in black who had given him the muttered warning back in Flagstaff? There was no telling. It seemed to make no sense for anyone to track him, but there were many possibilities, too many to think about.

Since the following rider did not seem to be gaining any ground and did not seem to intend to, Laredo tugged his hat lower against the sun, and rode on across the flats toward Bisbee, his horse laboring under him.

⋆　⋆　⋆

Twilight found Laredo on the outskirts of Bisbee, Arizona, which was also undergoing some kind of building boom, although with less lumber available than in Flagstaff, most of the new establishments had been thrown up using adobe-brick technology. A few had been daubed with whitewash, and some of these had signs hanging from their eaves advertising hopeful enterprises. Laredo rode to the center of town and passed the sheriff's office. Undoubtedly, Radcliffe had gone home to supper, but there appeared to be a deputy inside. A lantern burned behind the window set in its yellow brick wall, and two horses were tied to the pole rail in front.

Laredo was not in urgent need of

the sheriff, so he walked his horse on until he came to a stable. It had an amazingly low roof for such an establishment, and he saw he could not ride through the double doors. He swung down in front of the pole-and-adobe building, noticing a pen outside on the far side of the stable where a variety of horseflesh mingled. A few of these came closer to watch his approach, perhaps expecting the return of their usual riders.

As Laredo approached the doors, a squat little man with a patch over one eye, wearing homespun trousers and a badly cracked leather vest, watched him. Laredo greeted the man casually and got a muttered reply.

'I need to feed and stable my gray,' Laredo said. 'We've been riding long, so you'll have to be careful how much water you give him at first.'

'It looks to be in good shape to me,' the little man said in a disagreeable tone as he ran his hand over the gray's flank.

'I'm just asking you to make sure he doesn't bloat,' Laredo said.

'I believe I know how to take care of horses after twenty years on the job,' the man said, his good eye flashing. Laredo decided to appease him.

'I'm sure you do. I just thought I'd let you know that he hasn't had much water for a long while.'

'I'll see to him,' the stubby man promised. Laredo could now smell the raw whiskey on him. The stableman led the gray away and began removing its saddle. Laredo fished in his pocket and counted his silver.

'How much for the night and the feed?' he asked.

'Mostly men pay when they come back for their horses — those who do.'

'I know I'm coming back, and I know it's just going to be a single night,' Laredo told him. The stable-hand's good eye glinted with faint avarice as he looked at the coins in Laredo's palm. Perhaps the business wasn't doing all that well.

'Fifty cents for stabling, fifty cents for hay.'

'And I want him to have a bait of oats,' Laredo said.

'Make it a dollar and a quarter,' the stableman said, throwing Laredo's saddle over a stall partition.

'Let's make it two dollars,' Laredo said, slipping the man a pair of silver cartwheels. 'You might as well curry-comb him if that'll cover it.'

'That'll do me,' the one-eyed man said eagerly.

'One other thing — you don't mind if I hang around here for a while, do you? I was waiting to see if a friend of mine trails in.'

'Mister, since you're paying up front, I don't care if you stay here all night.' He paused. 'As a matter of fact, you could do me a favor — I need to go up town for just a few minutes. Could you just watch the place in case someone comes by? Tell them I'll be right back.'

'Sure,' Laredo agreed. He had no doubt where the man was headed.

There was a saloon just across the street.

The stable-hand wasted no time in scooting toward it. Laredo was left to lead his own horse into a stall, see that it had fresh hay and water, and return to stand in the shadows by the doorway, watching for the man who had been following him all the way from Flagstaff.

Minutes passed with no sound but the occasional dissatisfied blowing of a horse or the noisy passing of men exiting the saloon. It was half an hour or so before the one-eyed man returned, a brown paper sack in the shape of a bottle in his hand.

'Sorry,' he apologized, 'I got held up.'

'It's all right. I was in no hurry,' Laredo said.

'I guess your friend didn't show up, then?' the stableman asked, squinting with his single eye.

'No. It doesn't matter.' Laredo shouldered his saddle-bags and stepped out into the gathering gloom of night.

He hadn't been in Bisbee for quite a while, but he thought he could find his way to the hotel. A night's sleep in a bed would be a welcome luxury.

Making his way along the street the sounds from the saloons — the mock hilarity, the playful insults — drifted past like a fitful breeze. It was odd the way men choose to make their fun, he thought. But in these Western towns there was little else to do but drink and gamble. He thought he spotted the hotel standing on the corner of two intersecting streets ahead of him. White, two-storied, its lighted lamps beckoned to him from out of the darkness. Laredo's thoughts were only on whether he should eat first and then try to find a room, or check in first and eat later.

'Say, friend,' a voice called from the alley he was passing, 'could you spare a minute to help me out? I need to get this wheel back on my buggy.'

Laredo hesitated. In his time he had made the mistake of trying to assist someone who had something else in mind. But then again, how can you refuse to help a man who needs a hand? Such things were not done in his world, in the West.

'All right,' Laredo said, stepping into the alleyway. He knew almost immediately that he had made a mistake, for no disabled buggy stood there. Before he could back away from the set-up, however, heavy arms were thrown around him, pinning his arms to his side. All Laredo could do was think, 'Never again' as a second man stepped out of the shadows and drove his fist into Laredo's stomach.

The blow was hard, driving the breath from Laredo. He was only grateful that his stomach had been empty for a long while as nausea swept over him. The man holding him from behind now drove his knee up, catching Laredo solidly behind his own knee, buckling his leg. The man in front swung his fists in a rhythmic, jackhammer way, spinning Laredo's head from side to side with each blow. Laredo tried to duck, to swivel, to kick out at his assailant, but it was a futile effort. They had him good and proper.

Laredo caught a sharp blow on his jaw, then one above his eye as he squirmed and tried to fight back. Then the man went to work on his ribs. Soon Laredo's head began to spin crazily and his body had stopped transmitting pain to his brain. He now heard the blows more than felt them. Still, enough of his brain was alert enough to wonder — what did they want?

Under these circumstances Laredo would have expected to hear the usual threats and warnings: 'Get out of town! Stay away from . . . ' But these men said nothing, issued no threats. Nor had they grabbed for his wallet or saddle-bags. It seemed a senseless beating by strangers, but Laredo did not think it was that. Soon he lost his ability to consider any of the possibilities. Unconsciousness was embracing him. He felt the big man's arms come free of him, heard a muted voice pant, as they let him slump to the ground, 'He's had enough', heard muffled footsteps shuffling away.

There was nothing left but the cold darkness. When Laredo managed to pry his eyes open long minutes — or was it hours? — later, he found this world little different from the one he had fallen into in his unconsciousness.

All was still; all was dark. The only noticeable change was that pain racked his body and his head was hammering with sick-making aches. It was no improvement at all from lying unconscious in the cold alley. Lying on his back, peering upward between the two rows of buildings flanking him, he could make out a single bright star and a cluster of dimmer ones like handmaidens all looking down at him with astral interest.

Laredo shook himself mentally — he could not actually shake his head without his skull erupting with violent pain. This was no time to indulge himself with star-fantasies; it was time to rise and continue on his way before he caught pneumonia stretched out on the cold alley floor.

Or before the men came back.

That was a possibility. Why they should he did not know, but then he had no idea why he had been jumped in the first place. He clawed his way across the oily surface of the alley toward the wall of the nearest building where he managed to pull himself up to a sitting position. He sat there with his head spinning violently, trying to find a way to breathe which did not bring pain to his battered ribs.

Making the great effort he turned, looked up at the wall and dragged himself painfully to his feet. He stood erect, head bowed to the wall, trying to regain some normal sense of balance and muscular control. His saddle-bags lay on the ground not ten feet from where he stood, and he wondered if it was worth going after them. Bending over might send him toppling over again back onto the ground. What would he lose if he left them where they were? Very little, but he moved toward them on unsteady legs and picked them up, shouldering them in a way an arthritic old man would not have envied.

His legs were wobbling. The night had grown cold and he shivered and shook. His hair was in his eyes; his eyes were filled with pain. Hat also recovered, he started toward the head of the alley with his Colt in his hand. They would not jump him again on this night, not without savage retribution.

* * *

Morning was bright, cool with only a few high, wind-flagged clouds streaking the deep blue of the sky. Laredo saw this as he bent and peered out of his hotel window. He knew he had somehow staggered to the hotel and checked in while curious eyes studied his battered face, torn shirt and dirty clothing, but he could remember little of it. His head had been a disturbed hive filled with angry hornets.

It was not much better on this morning.

Laredo sagged onto the bed, hands folded, and spent long minutes staring at the wall. His right eye was puffed and partially closed. There was a narrow thread of dried blood running down his forehead. He knew this without rising, going to the oval mirror over the washbasin. He had been avoiding the mirror, avoiding rising to his feet.

He had not dressed, had not needed to: apparently he had not undressed the night before. He had slept on top of the blue blanket on the bed, which explained the chill in his bones. Laredo knew who he was, where he was, but only vaguely why he had come there. It came back in chunks, like heavy sections of an iron puzzle clanking together.

He had wanted to talk to Glen Radcliffe and see what the sheriff knew about the horse trader, Randall Nye, who might have had dealings with one of the Red Butte boys. Still Laredo did not rise from his bed. He stared at the window where the glass shone dull blue and bright yellow in the morning light. Outside he could hear the sounds of men up and busy going about their daily routines. Finally, with a sigh, he rose and stomped to the washbasin.

He tried to avoid looking at his battered face as he washed; he tried to avoid touching the bruises with his fingers. Shaving, he decided, was out of the question. He looked mournfully at his stained and torn blue shirt. It was nearly new and had been one of his favorites. Fortunately he did have a spare shirt, an ox-blood red flannel one with black buttons. It was wrinkled from riding in his saddle-bags, but he struggled into it, his shoulders and ribs complaining with every movement.

Dressed, his face haphazardly washed, hair combed back, he sat down again on the bed. There had to be a better line of work — though truthfully he did not know if his job was the reason behind the beating he had taken. It could have been something as simple as mistaken identity in the darkness of the alley. Somehow he did not think so. He remembered that there had been no threat, no warning.

It did not matter: it was time to get to work. He found his hat on the floor, formed it as well as he could, planted it on his head and went out.

From somewhere on the block he could smell bacon and eggs frying; the thought of eating turned his stomach although he knew he should grab a breakfast. That would hold until later; first he would speak with Sheriff Radcliffe. Walking along the plank-walks, he found the saloons already lively with the forced mirth of early-morning drinkers. He glanced into one such establishment as he passed and saw a line of men standing near the bar still waiting for the alcohol to deliver their morning wake-up. They had pouched, dark-ringed eyes and a softness about them as if they had weakened their skeletons the night before. Others, further advanced on the new day, hooted at unlikely jokes or played desultory card games which no one ever won.

Laredo continued on his way, finding the sheriff's office standing alone in the sun like an unwanted blemish on the face of the town. He shouldered through the door and found Glen Radcliffe at his desk. The sheriff looked up with suspicion — a force of habit with lawmen. Every time someone came through the door, it could mean trouble and usually did. Radcliffe had his hat off which was unusual. He was under thirty years of age, but had lost his hair early. He now had only a few downy clumps of reddish hair covering his freckled scalp. His compensating mustache was a great, drooping red curtain drawn across his upper lip.

'What can I do for you ... ?'

Radcliffe began and then hesitated, recognizing Laredo despite the year since their last meeting, despite the battered aspect of the tall man who had entered. 'Laredo?' he said, coming to his feet in one easy motion.

'It's me. I'm surprised you recognize me.'

'Your own mother might not recognize you, Laredo. You look like you were entered in a kicking contest with a mule.'

'They didn't give me much of a chance,' Laredo said, seating himself gingerly in a straight-backed wooden chair.

'Is that why you're here? To file a complaint?' Radcliffe asked, settling into his chair again. A lanky, red-faced deputy came through the front door then with a tray covered with a checked cloth. From the smell, Laredo judged it to be breakfast for the prisoners. The deputy crossed the office with barely a glance at Laredo.

'I couldn't if I wanted to,' Laredo

admitted. 'I don't know who they were, what they looked like. They jumped me in a dark alley.'

'You have any idea why?'

'None,' Laredo had to tell the sheriff. 'So that doesn't leave you with a lot to investigate, does it?'

'No,' the sheriff said. 'Then what is it that brings you here, Laredo?'

'I am following up on the Mountain Springs robbery,' Laredo told him and the sheriff's eyes darkened, not with anger, but with amusement.

'You are some kind of damned fool, Laredo,' Radcliffe said, telling Laredo something he already knew. He knew it, but it was a little too late for him to change now.

3

Glen Radcliffe had planted his wide-brimmed straw hat on his bald skull and with his fierce-appearing red mustache now looked the part of a tough, no-nonsense lawman. He had folded his hands together on his belly, propped his boots up on the desk and eyed Laredo steadily, frowning all the time.

'You give me cause to recall a story,' Radcliffe said.

Laredo leaned back in his chair and waited. Glen Radcliffe was well known for his stories; sometimes it was difficult to catch the moral of them. The office had begun to warm with the day; a fly walked across the desk. In the back of the jail, the deputy was yelling something at the prisoners. Apparently they didn't appreciate their breakfast enough.

'Go on,' Laredo coaxed, knowing that he was going to hear it whether he wanted to or not.

'It concerns a Texas cattleman who was interviewing two men for a job. One of them was a smart, educated Easterner. The other was a man of the West.' Laredo only nodded and Radcliffe continued. ''Boys,' the cattleman said, 'I need someone to ride through to Colorado to talk to a man who wants to buy a hundred head of my beef.'

'The Easterner, he asks, 'How long will it take me? Is there good water along the trail, grass for my horse? Will I need a spare pony? Are there any towns along the way, trading posts to buy necessities at? I've heard that the Indians have been making a fuss up that way; is it true? I assume you won't want me going before it quits snowing.'

'When the rancher asked the man of the West, his reply was, 'Where in Colorado?''

'I'm not sure I get you,' Laredo said. 'Don't you? You're like that Western man I'm speaking of. They give you an impossible job and all you ask is to be pointed in the right direction. Laredo,' Radcliffe said with a sigh, 'the Mountain Springs hold-up was ten years ago. Not only was I not sheriff here, I was too young to have been a lawman. Yet here you are trying to track those men down.'

'It's the job I was given,' Laredo shrugged. Then he asked, 'What can you tell me about a man named Randall Nye?'

'Nye? What has he got to do with this?'

'I wish I could be sure,' Laredo said, and he proceeded to tell the sheriff how Nye was said to have come by one of the stolen gold certificates.

'You don't seem too certain about his explanation,' Radcliffe said.

'I'm far from accusing the man of anything,' Laredo answered, 'but the thought has crossed my mind that Nye could be one of the Red Butte boys using another name. He may have concocted the tale of the horse deal gone bad just to try to pass the gold certificate.'

The deputy sheriff tramped back in from the back cells just then, the serving tray still in his hands. He was complaining. 'You can't do anything to please those boys back there. Here we give them breakfast on the county's tab and they don't eat it — just make rude remarks. What can you do when their entire diet usually consists of whiskey? They hate to waste money on food, and don't know how to eat it if it doesn't come out of a bottle.'

'All right, Earl. We tried,' Radcliffe said in a soothing tone. He was obviously used to hearing his deputy's complaints. 'I'll cut them loose this afternoon. You won't have to take any more guff off them.'

The deputy, Earl, only nodded, shouldered his way through the front door and went off grumbling.

'I love my job,' Radcliffe said sardonically. 'You know, Laredo, if I had the room for them, I could lock up half the town every night for drinking and fighting. You have to get pretty obnoxious to get yourself locked up in Bisbee.'

'It's that way pretty much everywhere,' Laredo commented. 'There's no revenue in it. But to get back to business . . . '

'What do I know about Randall Nye,' Radcliffe said, with a nod of his head. He tilted his hat back, showing a little more bare scalp. 'Very little actually. His business as a horse trader keeps him on the move. There was a time when he went in for mustanging, but the wild horses were more trouble to break and train than they were worth, so he moved on to selling saddle stock. He purchased a lot of them from down-and-out cowboys, fattened the animals up and sold them at a higher price. Now and then he got hold of some bloodstock. He had one good Kentucky stallion that flopped in a short race with a Quarter Horse out here, which any fool could have told him would happen. The dissatisfied owner sold it to Nye for a quarter of what it was worth. The man, it seemed, was furious. He had lost a lot of money on that race.

'After the man cooled down he tried to buy it back, but of course the price had doubled.' Radcliffe shrugged. 'I have no knowledge of Nye ever doing anything flat illegal — though some of his ethics might make a Baptist minister shudder a little.'

Laredo said, 'One man's crook is another man's smart horse trader.'

'Exactly. I haven't seen Nye for quite some time, maybe six months or so. He has a little place about ten miles east of town. Not much, really, but it has a stream running through it. A good enough place to hold horses temporarily, which he uses it for, but no place you'd want to raise a family. Nye isn't there often — his business keeps the man moving around a lot.'

'I'll probably ride out that way,'

Laredo said. 'I have to start somewhere.' He asked the sheriff, 'There's never been any talk of Nye rustling horses, has there?'

'No. Not that I've ever heard. He's just a damn sharp horse dealer who has gotten the best of every man he's traded with.'

'Except one,' Laredo reminded the lawman, 'the man with the stolen gold certificate — if he exists.'

Laredo got to his feet and reached for his hat. Radcliffe did not bother to rise. He was probably resting up for another night spent policing Bisbee's rowdy saloons.

'The barbershop up the street has leeches, Laredo, unless you're squeamish about them. That eye of yours is going to close up all the way if you don't do something about it.'

'I don't like the thought of leeches much,' Laredo admitted, 'but I guess I'll have to give it a try. Thanks.'

'One other thought, Laredo: it's not really a good idea to go around fighting two men at once unless you really happen to need the exercise.'

Laredo half-smiled, nodded and went out into the sun-bright streets of Bisbee. He went first to the barbershop to get his bruised, cut and whiskered face worked on. He tipped the man for the decent job he did. Then he went across the street and picked out two new shirts and a pair of black jeans. Removing the clothing that had been torn and muddied in the fight bolstered his sense of well-being.

Barbered and dressed in clean clothes, Laredo felt much better about himself as he approached the Bank of Bisbee, where Jake Royle had told him a line of credit had been established for him. He would need cash for supplies, he knew, and, after thinking it over further, he withdrew several hundred dollars. He might have to present himself as a horse buyer if he were to manage to have a talk with the elusive Randall Nye.

As of now, Nye was his only possible

lead to the Red Butte gang and the stolen gold certificates.

Completing his business at the bank, Laredo returned to the hotel to retrieve his belongings. The window to his room was cracked open an inch or two and the light curtains fluttered in the dry breeze. Despite this ventilation there was the scent of smoke in the room. The bed was still unmade, and so no maid had been there yet. His gear all seemed to be where he had stowed it, but lifting a hand to the lamp on the wall, he could feel the lingering warmth on the glass chimney with his fingertips. Someone had been there while he was gone, and whoever it was had not long since departed. A matter of minutes only.

Frowning, Laredo considered matters. He walked to the window. From there a lookout could see him returning to the hotel and give warning to someone else who would quit what he was doing and extinguish the lamp. But what would they have been looking for?

And who were they?

Of course, it could be no more complicated than that the hotel had its share of burglars. There were people who preyed on travelers in most hotels. That could be it, but Laredo was not your ordinary traveler.

He had already been beaten for no apparent reason. And there was the man in black he had encountered in Flagstaff, the one who had warned him off. Had he, or another interested party, trailed him to Bisbee? He was almost certain that someone had been riding on his back trail. What did they want? Were they looking for a badge, a list of names, a clue to the whereabouts of the stolen money?

All of these were worth considering, but Laredo believed none of them implicitly. At any rate there was no sense in pondering these notions now. First he searched through his belongings. His saddle-bags seemed to have been rifled, but this was far from certain after what they had been through. Gathering his gear, he went out again into the brilliant sunlight to retrieve his gray horse from the stable.

He asked the young, dark man who saddled his horse, 'Ever hear of a man named Randall Nye?'

The stable-hand's head swiveled slowly toward Laredo. His dark eyes narrowed with suspicion.

'Sure, my boss deals with him sometimes,' he answered grudgingly. 'They trade horses, buy and sell.' The man let go of the near stirrup and it flapped down with finality.

'Do you know where I might find Nye?' Laredo persisted.

The man shook his head. 'You might find him anywhere, I suppose, but I don't know. It's my boss, not me, who has dealings with him. Personally I wouldn't . . . I don't know, mister.'

There was obviously no more the man knew or was going to tell, so Laredo thanked him, led the gray out of the dark confines of the stable and swung on to the saddle. It seemed there was little to learn in Bisbee about Nye that he didn't already know. Radcliffe had told him that there was some sort of ranch where Nye sometimes held his wild stock ten miles east of town. Laredo tugged his hat low against the glare of the sun and hit the eastern trail.

★　★　★

The day was warm and dry before Laredo came upon the ranch, seen through a screen of cottonwood trees. He halted the big gray horse and studied Nye's set-up. Removing his hat, Laredo mopped his brow. The day was not uncomfortable, but it was warm enough to start the perspiration flowing.

Randall Nye's ranch was not what Laredo had expected from the way Sheriff Radcliffe had described it. Maybe the sheriff hadn't been by for a while. After all, besides keeping order in Bisbee, there was over 6,000 square miles of Cochise County to be patrolled.

Along the stream flowing through the grassy meadow there were dozens of horses. The buildings, set back from the river, which might have had a tendency to flood, were low and long. One must be the main house, the other two perhaps bunkhouses. There had been no plan in the construction of these, and they seemed to have been built at different times; however, Laredo was forced to disagree with Sheriff Radcliffe's negative appraisal of Nye's ranch. Certainly hundreds of struggling ranchers would have envied the place.

Again, maybe Radcliffe had not seen the ranch as it was now. Laredo waited in the shade of the trees, in no hurry to ride down. For the moment he enjoyed the breeze through the trees, the sight of grazing horses along the silver-blue river. He must have waited a little too long, for a voice boomed out from behind him.

'Who are you and what are you doing

here? No — don't turn your head toward me. Just answer the questions!'

'I'm looking for Randall Nye — is that you?'

'Do I look like Randall Nye?' his visitor growled.

'I wouldn't know. You told me not to turn my head; besides, I've never seen Nye.' Laredo heard a horse being walked nearer, its hoofs crackling the dry leaves underfoot.

'Who are you and what do you want here?' the man demanded again.

'Horses are my business,' Laredo said, and now that he had had a moment to scrape a name up, he told his questioner, 'My name's Larry Cotton.' It probably didn't matter if the man knew his real name or not, but Laredo decided to play it safe.

'You're not from around here,' the man said with deeper suspicion in his voice.

'No, I'm not. Nobody has any horses for sale where I'm from. I decided to come where the horses were. Everyone says Nye is the man to see. Is he around right now?'

'I don't like your smell,' the stranger said, and Laredo wondered what had caused his dislike and suspicion. He couldn't have mistaken Laredo for a horse thief, not a lone man who already had a mount of his own. Perhaps it was the way Laredo wore his gun or the clothes he was wearing. There was no telling; maybe the man was just plain suspicious and didn't like anyone.

'I think you'd better come on down to the ranch with me,' the man said.

'That was my intention all along. Is Nye on the property? I heard he travels a lot.'

'You hear a lot for a stranger. Who told you about Randall Nye?'

Laredo didn't think it was a good idea to bring up Glenn Radcliffe's name and so he answered, 'Some boys at the stable in town. They said Nye was the man to talk to if I was looking for horses.'

'The stable has more than a few

horses of its own.'

'I saw them; I didn't like the looks of any of them much. I thought it'd be to my advantage to see what kind of stock Nye had.'

'You know what, stranger,' the man said, 'you do too much thinking.'

'Yeah, maybe. You haven't told me if Nye is on the place.'

'If he is, I don't know as he'll want to see you.'

'Funny way to do business,' Laredo said.

'Well, Randall Nye, he does his business his own way, and with who he wishes. Now start that horse of yours, mister. I'm taking you down to the ranch.'

The man still had not allowed Laredo a glimpse of his face. He had the overly cautious manner of an outlaw, though. From his voice Laredo guessed that his age was about right for the men he was seeking. Was it possible the entire Red Butte gang was quartered at this lonely ranch? Laredo wanted to have a look at the man's face. Although he had never seen any of the robbers and the descriptions he had gotten from Jake Royle were pretty vague, still several of them had identifying marks that they could not hide. Stoker, for example, had a scar running vertically across his left eye. Winslow Pear, it was said, was missing three toes on his right foot. Asa Taylor was said to weigh about 250 pounds. Of course he could have lost weight in the intervening years — or gained more.

Laredo could also think of no good reason why all of the outlaws would have come up from Mexico after their years spent in comfort and safety down there, but then as his escort had told him, Laredo was prone to doing too much thinking.

And coming up with too few answers.

They had left the shade of the trees and now rode down the sunny slope of a dry grass knoll toward the larger of the houses, the one on his right. The man riding with Laredo had not spoken again to him except to tell him which way to go. Once, turned only slightly in his saddle, Laredo had been able to see a square-shouldered man of middle years riding a paint pony, his rifle across the saddle bow. No details of the man's face were visible during that short glance.

'Tie up in front,' Laredo was instructed.

'Is Nye here?' Laredo asked, but he was not answered.

Somehow, some way, Laredo was about to get some of his many questions answered inside that house. He didn't know if they would be answered in the way he might have wished.

4

Laredo swung down from his gray and tied up at the rail. The man with the rifle stepped down as well. Along the riverbank two colts were engaged in an impromptu race. The glint of the sun was brilliant on the flowing water. No one else seemed to be about to enjoy the day. As he waited for his escort, Laredo found himself wondering idly if Dusty would have liked this place. Dusty, his wife. His patient, redheaded, cheerful wife who was at home in the town of Crater, Arizona, who made him laugh and made the finest shoofly pie in the territory. Each time he left her, he wondered if he would return. Laredo knew he did not have to work; Dusty had inherited much wealth, but they both knew that Laredo could not be kept at home to rot away in a rocking chair, so as much as Dusty disliked his profession, she cut him free to do what he was called upon to do . . .

'Go on in!' he was commanded. 'What are you waiting for?'

'For you to tell me what to do.'

'I'm telling you now.' Laredo turned toward the door to the house. 'Call out,' he was ordered.

'Coming in!' Laredo announced. Obviously, then, there was someone waiting inside.

The front room had a low ceiling, a large stone fireplace and smelled of old tobacco smoke. There were no furnishings but a puncheon wood couch with red and green striped cushions and a matching high-backed chair. The walls were an undecorated flat white. Laredo felt the floorboards creak, heard boot leather over the wood as someone slipped up behind him.

A hand was clamped over his left arm and another pawed at his holster. 'We'll take that gun,' the man said.

Laredo threw his elbow back sharply, catching the man in the windpipe, and his attacker stepped away choking. 'No, you won't,' Laredo said and he changed his position so that his back was near the wall and he had a clear view of the three men in the room. He had not drawn his pistol, but he was ready enough.

'Look, gents,' Laredo said, with his voice dropping to something like menace, 'I came here horse-shopping. If you plain just don't like strangers around, step aside and I'll leave. It's not worth it to me. And it won't be worth it to you if you try any funny stuff with me.'

The plank door through which they had entered still stood open and now Laredo had a good look at the three rough men standing around him in a loose half-circle. The one who had brought him to the house was a flat-faced man in blue jeans and a dark-blue shirt. He still carried his rifle.

The second one stood near the cold fireplace. He was bulky, squat, powerful-appearing. The third, the one

Laredo had staggered with his elbow, was narrow with thinning red hair and a sneer which seemed to be his constant expression. He spoke to Laredo.

'You're not telling us what to do. Not in this house.'

'Your house, is it?' Laredo asked, his hand now resting on the butt of his holstered pistol.

'No, it belongs to Randall Nye, but we work here.'

'It looks like you put in some tough days.'

'Shut up,' said the man with the rifle who seemed to be in charge. 'Look, mister, maybe we made a mistake. We were just trying to protect the property, you know. Why don't we just forget it?'

'Where's Nye?' Laredo asked, glancing around the room. A short corridor led off somewhere to his right; probably the bedrooms were back there. To his left there was an entranceway to an open kitchen.

'He's not here right now,' the man

61

with the rifle answered. He had now lowered his weapon to hold it loosely in his right hand, meaning he was left-handed, Laredo thought. For to bring a rifle to bear for a right-handed man it was more natural to hold it in his left. That was his thought, for whatever it was worth. He was there to observe and while he had the chance, he meant to use it.

The man with the rifle and the flat, round face wore a black handlebar mustache. The facial hair meant nothing — it comes and goes. Laredo still had not seen anything that he could match up with the descriptions of any of the Mountain Springs robbers. Perhaps there was nothing to be discovered. These men might have had nothing to do with any of that.

He had noticed one thing, however: the flat-faced man's voice was familiar. Not definitely so, but it sounded much like the voice he had heard in the alleyway last night when he was beaten. He could recognize none of them from that event either. It had just been too dark. He glanced at the stocky man built like a no-holds-barred wrestler, who stood with his back to the fireplace, expressionless. He would have liked to have seen that one's hands to look for bruises and cuts, but he had them behind his back.

Thinking of that episode, Laredo had to wonder again why they had picked him to beat on. It had hardly seemed to be a random assault. It had to be someone who wanted him — Laredo — specifically warned off. For those men who had no idea who he was to have selected Laredo as a target they must have had him pointed out by someone who did know Laredo. Who?

'All right,' the rifleman said after a silent conference with his two friends, 'You'd better get out of here. Randall Nye isn't here, and I don't know when he'll be back. The man travels a lot.'

'Do you mind if I look over the horses he's got?' Laredo asked, playing out his role of horse buyer to the end.

'Wouldn't do you no good, not with Nye away. Look, mister, find some other place that's got horses for sale. I don't want to see you hanging around here any longer, and I don't want you coming back for any reason, do you understand?'

'Not really, but if that's the way things are — '

'That's the way things are. Climb aboard that horse of yours and make tracks out of here before I change my mind.'

There was nothing else to be done at the moment, and so, with a glance at the two men flanking him, Laredo strode across the floor toward the bright rectangle of the open door.

Laredo rode back carefully toward Bisbee, his eyes searching the land around him and occasionally the trail behind him. He had learned nothing. In fact he had more questions than he had before riding to Nye's ranch.

There was no way he was going to be able to solve this case. It was just . . .

impossible. He smiled as he thought of Jake Royle's sad reaction to Laredo's use of the word, but if there was a way to even get a handle on this, it eluded Laredo.

In Bisbee he encountered Glen Radcliffe in the restaurant called Blue Belle's where the sheriff was just finishing up his dinner. Radcliffe glanced up as Laredo approached his table and gestured for him to take a seat.

'The lamb stew's good and the cornbread is fresh,' he told Laredo.

'I don't favor lamb,' Laredo said, seating himself. Radcliffe shrugged.

'Well, they always burn a good steak here.' He lifted his eyes. 'Have any luck today?'

'Not so's you'd notice,' Laredo had to tell him.

'Rode out to Randall Nye's, did you?'

'I did. Nye wasn't there.'

Radcliffe nodded. 'I told you the man moves around a lot.' Laredo ordered a steak and potatoes from the thin blonde waitress who skittered up to the table and smiled at Radcliffe.

'He's got himself a nice little set-up out there,' Laredo commented. 'Room for six or a dozen men.'

'Does he now? He must have been working on it since I last visited,' Radcliffe said. 'Is anyone around there now?'

'I met three men, not very friendly types. There may have been more around, I don't know. These boys claimed to be ranch hands, but they were standing idle in the middle of the day.'

'Well, when the boss is away . . . ' the sheriff said. He leaned back in his chair, picking his teeth. The waitress brought his check and took some change from the sheriff. 'Thank you, Mabel,' Radcliffe said and got another smile from the girl. 'Nice girl,' Radcliffe said to Laredo after she was gone, 'not much meat on her, though . . .

'So, you don't think the three men you met were ranch hands. What do you take them for, Laredo?'

'I don't know,' he said honestly.

'But you're thinking about it.'

'I'm thinking about it, but not getting far.' Laredo removed his arms from the table so that Mabel, the returning waitress, could serve his platter. As he did so he happened to shift his gaze to the far side of the room.

'Who's that, Glen?'

'Who?' Glen swiveled in his chair to look in the direction Laredo was indicating.

Studying the pale stranger in the black suit seated at the far table, Radcliffe could put no name to the face. 'I have no idea, Laredo. Why, is it important?'

'I wish I knew,' Laredo said, cutting his meat.

He did wish he knew because the man in the black suit with the high stiff collar resembled the man in black who had tried to warn him off back in Flagstaff. His suit was hardly a trailsman's style of dress, and he could have had it brushed and cleaned since trailing Laredo down across the open land . . . if it was the same man. Laredo had never gotten a clear look at the man's face back in Bisbee.

'Just somebody I thought I'd seen before. I thought you might know him.'

'No,' Radcliffe said, shaking his head. 'He's not from around here, that's all I can tell you.'

'It probably doesn't matter,' Laredo said. 'Maybe I'm developing a case of the jitters.'

Radcliffe stood, put a hand briefly on Laredo's shoulder. 'You're looking too hard for solutions where there may not be any. I'll be back at the office in about an hour if you want to talk about something else.'

Laredo nodded, his mouth filled with a bite of beefsteak. Did he want to talk more? About what? Maybe within the hour he or Glen Radcliffe would come up with a few meaningful questions if not answers. For now Laredo felt that he was jousting with ghosts, chasing insubstantial robbers — who might not even still exist ten years after the hold-up at Mountain Springs and flight to Mexico.

The only clue he had had was Randall Nye and his supposed meeting with the horse buyer. Now Randall Nye was gone somewhere and the buyer with the $500 gold bond might be nothing more than an imaginary witness. It wasn't a lot to base an investigation on.

Well, he had known from the beginning that this case was not going to be easy. Laredo pushed his plate away, meal unfinished, eyed the man in the black suit who seemed to be paying him no attention now.

Laredo paid for his bill, leaving a tip for Mabel, who gave him a smile of thanks. It was a nice smile, a shy smile, but definitely not the same sort as she had given Sheriff Radcliffe. With his dinner only a settling memory, Laredo stepped out into the bright sunlight of the Arizona day and was faced with a would-be killer.

Glen Radcliffe was still on the plankwalk in front of the restaurant, speaking with two townspeople. Along the street a man who seemed to have an injured leg dragged his way toward them, his eyes fixed on Laredo. As he neared them Laredo could see that those eyes were overbright, and what he had taken for an injured gait was the result of alcohol unsteadiness. The man was drunk and swaying, but focused entirely on his work.

Beside him Laredo saw the sheriff move the two townsmen aside with his arm. They scuttled away toward shelter, one going inside the restaurant, the other into the nearby alley.

'No you don't, Poge!' Radcliffe yelled at the approaching man, whom he obviously knew. 'Go away! Get another drink or pass out somewhere, but go away.'

'Move aside, Sheriff. It's not you I want,' a slurred, curiously high-pitched voice, answered. 'I'll have that *hombre* with you step out into the street. It's something I'm bound to do.'

The man had determination in his voice, and he carried his pistol like he knew what it was for. Laredo stepped into the street and forward, trying to talk sense to the drunk. That is usually an exercise bound to fail, and it did this time. The spirits in Poge's mind urged him on not with reason, but with relentless goading.

'Look, friend,' Laredo said, halting and bracing himself when Poge had gotten to within twenty steps of him, 'this is unnecessary.'

'So you say,' Poge yelled back. 'A man has to earn his pay, don't he?'

Radcliffe had come up beside Laredo now, on his left side, and he tried to mollify the drunken man. 'Listen, Poge, back off. We'll talk about it later. This man is a friend of mine, and I — '

Poge, who had not been listening to a word of the sheriff's caution, went for his gun as Laredo shoved Radcliffe roughly aside and drew his own Colt, rolling to the ground. The bullet Poge had fired flew past Laredo and slammed into an upright support post of the restaurant's awning, spraying splinters. A second shot was loosed as Laredo continued to roll. This one missed as well, but it was so near that the bullet covered Laredo's face with dust. That was enough.

Laredo came to one knee and sighted. His first shot stopped Poge in his tracks and sent him staggering. The second one caught him low and doubled him over, dropping his weapon as he clutched at his belly.

No third shot was necessary. Poge stumbled forward two more steps, said something to the gods of the Arizona sky and pitched forward on his face to die in the middle of the dusty street.

Shakily Laredo got to his feet. Glen Radcliffe, gun in his hands, was already by Poge's body checking it for signs of life.

Laredo approached slowly. He had never liked the sight of a man whose breath had departed his body, especially not when he was the one who had extinguished the spark of life.

'Who was he?' Laredo asked a tight-lipped Radcliffe.

'Byron Poge,' Glen answered. 'A local fast gun artist. He never moved up high on the list of known gunmen because he hadn't the heart for it. He had to get himself soaked in liquor to get the nerve to take a man on. When he was sober, I never saw a man quicker and more accurate than Byron Poge. The thing was, he was never sober for long at a time.

'When he was sober,' Radcliffe said, looking down at the body, 'you never saw his like. No offense, Laredo, but I doubt when he was sober if you could have ever taken Byron Poge on your best day.'

Laredo said, 'Then I thank the curse of hard liquor.'

Radcliffe was directing a couple of men to take the body away and do whatever they did with the departed in

Bisbee. Laredo had retreated to the shade of the restaurant's awning. On the heels of the violent encounter, he had a case of the jitters. His body actually trembled for a long minute. It was not a new occurrence to Laredo; he did not try to disguise it. He thought of himself as a good recovery operative, but he never had had the makings of a killer.

'You got him good,' the feminine, Spanish voice at his side said with a hiss. 'He was never so good as Speed, but very dangerous, no? You get them all in some time.'

'Speed?' he asked, turning to look down at a short, dark girl in a waitress's outfit. 'Who do you mean?'

'Who do I mean?' the girl with dancing brown eyes said. 'Harry Speed. Who do you think?'

Harry Speed? Of the Red Butte gang? The outlaw with the reputation of being one of the fastest guns in the territory as well as being one of the members of the gang that had pulled off the

Mountain Springs robbery?

'I thought Harry Speed was dead — years ago,' Laredo said, feeling his way.

'Just nobody see him for years,' the small woman said with a half-laugh. ''Scuse me, I got to go back to work.'

'Wait, what's your name?' Laredo asked.

'Alicia,' the girl said, turning her eyes down after batting them, perhaps imagining that Laredo was flirting with her. Then she vanished into the clamor of Blue Belle's restaurant.

Laredo stood there in the heat for long minutes, letting his nerves calm, trying to assimilate what Alicia had just told him. Then he started on somberly toward Sheriff Glen Radcliffe's office as two men threw the body of Byron Poge dispassionately into the back of a wagon. The sky was coloring somewhat to the west. Sunset and the welcome cooling of the day would arrive soon.

5

'Well,' Radcliffe asked, when Laredo again entered the sheriff's office, 'are you feeling better?'

'My nerves are settled,' Laredo answered, taking a seat, removing his hat, 'but I can't say I'm feeling better about things. Killing seems never to be worth it, you must know that.'

'Unfortunately I do,' Glenn Radcliffe agreed. 'Even when it's necessary, it seems that it is not worth it, that there must have been another way.'

'You saw Poge's eyes. There wasn't any other way,' Laredo said. 'Who was Poge, exactly? What could have prompted him to come after me?'

'Poge was a small-time bully. He thought of himself as a gun for hire. The trouble was,' Radcliffe said, leaning back with his arms behind his head, 'nobody much hired him. He couldn't be trusted to stay sober long enough to finish the job.'

'Somebody didn't know that, or care. I know this was a kill-for-hire job. You heard him say 'A man's got to earn his pay.''

'Yes, I heard that,' Radcliffe said, shaking his head. 'Must have been someone who only knew him by reputation, not by effectiveness.'

'A stranger to Bisbee,' Laredo suggested.

'Might be — look, Laredo, you have someone in mind. Who do you think hired Poge?'

'The man in black,' Laredo said. He had no evidence to base that on. Only a strong suspicion. He would find the man and have a conversation with him. It was a wild idea, that the man had warned him in Flagstaff, trailed him all the way to Bisbee, and then hired a local gun to kill him. In fact it seemed incredible. Was Laredo only grasping at straws . . . ?

'Who is this Alicia who works at the

Blue Belle?' Laredo asked. 'A little Mexican girl.'

'A waitress, that's all I know,' Glen said, now leaning forward. 'Why do you ask?'

'She knows Harry Speed.'

'Harry — ' The sheriff bit at his thumbnail and shook his head. 'It isn't possible.'

'She says it is,' Laredo countered, then he went on to relate his conversation with the girl. Radcliffe listened carefully and shook his head again.

'I'll ask Mabel if she knows anything about the girl, where she came from, if she has a man friend. Those waitresses are a pretty chatty group.' Radcliffe sighed and then settled his eyes on Laredo again. Quite serious now, he asked, 'Laredo, are you sure you're not working at this too hard? Nye, Harry Speed, the man in black. Are you sure you're not trying too hard to solve this trouble with the Red Butte gang by weaving together a few loose threads?'

'No, I'm not sure,' Laredo said,

glancing toward the window where the sundown sky was coloring the world. 'But that's what I came here to try to do. It's what they pay me for.'

'Better you than me,' Radcliffe said with a frown.

From up the street near the saloons a voice could be heard shouting and a shot was fired. The sheriff reached for his hat. 'That's what they pay me to take care of,' he told Laredo as they walked toward the door. 'The nightly chorus of fun in Bisbee.' Another shot was fired from the direction of the saloons. Radcliffe looked unworried. 'They seldom do any real damage, just like pulling the trigger now and then. But, you never know.'

Laredo watched Radcliffe stride off toward the sounds of trouble — maybe his own job wasn't that bad. Having no place else to go, he started off toward the hotel, using the middle of the street this time. He hadn't yet stabled his horse, thinking he might ride again this night. The idea now seemed futile. He recovered the gray and walked it to the stable to have it put to bed.

Walking back an hour later he passed the Blue Belle, wondering if he ought to interview Alicia again. The trouble was, that would alert her and she might have the contacts to warn some of the men he wanted to find. He decided to return to his room, study the descriptions of the men in the Red Butte gang once again, committing them to memory, and then retire early. There just wasn't much else to be done.

Nor was there much that was productive he could do in the morning. He still needed to talk to Randall Nye, but the horse trader could be a hundred miles away. There was no guarantee that the man would even talk to him. Outside of that, the only thing Laredo could accomplish was to look for the pale man in black. There was really nothing to accuse him of: anyone could have had Laredo beaten up; anyone might have hired Poge to kill him; it could have been anyone following along back on the trail from Flagstaff, but that didn't mean that Laredo didn't want to find the man and look him over closely.

He knew before he had entered his room this time that someone had been again. There was a ribbon of lantern light showing under the door, and the door was not fully closed. Laredo stopped, looked around in the hall, and then eased toward the doorway, his hand resting on his Colt.

What had they come back for? If this was an ambush, it was a sloppy one.

The unlikely fragrance of lilac reached him as he prepared to shoulder open the door to his room, and when the door did swing to, he was surprised, but hardly astonished, to find the girl, Alicia, perched on his bed. A quick glance around assured him that she was the only one there.

'Hello, Laredo,' she said. In this light, hair freshly brushed, she looked like a pixie — a world-weary pixie, but a pixie nonetheless. She was wearing her yellow and white waitress's dress from the Blue Belle.

'How did you learn my name?' he asked, pulling out a wooden chair which he reversed to sit on facing her, his eyes flickering occasionally to the open door.

'Oh, Mabel she tell me. The Sheriff Radcliffe tell her,' the Mexican girl replied, struggling only a little with her English.

'I wonder why Glen did that.'

'Who is Glen? Oh, yes, the Sheriff Radcliffe,' Alicia said. 'He wants to know something so he asks Mabel. Mabel says she don't know nothing about me, so Mabel she says, 'You better go over and talk to the man Laredo before you get in some trouble.' So here I am.'

'Well, since you are here,' Laredo said, trying to keep his voice calm. He didn't want the girl excited. 'First of all, you're not in any trouble. I'm sorry you had to leave your job to come over here.'

Alicia shrugged and smiled, revealing even white teeth. 'You think I have so much fun serving dishes?'

'No. I just wouldn't want you to get in trouble with your boss.'

She shrugged again. 'Nobody cares. Me and Mabel are the two best girls, and Mabel says she will do my job. No one will even know I am gone. If so, Mabel says she will make up a story.' She raised her thin round arms and stretched them overhead. 'What is it you want? Are you going to shoot more men?' Her expression was almost eager.

'I don't know. I hope not. You said you know Harry Speed — he's the man I'm interested in right now.'

'Oh, don't go to shoot him!' Alicia said with a flicker of concern. 'He is a fast man with a gun — very fast.'

'You've seen him shoot?'

'Oh, yes,' the waitress said. Excitement was causing her accent to return a little. What she had said sounded more like 'Oh, jes.' 'Only just bottles and cans and rocks, but I saw him practice every day at our houses in Mexico.'

'You lived with Harry Speed?' Laredo asked.

'Oh no.' She tittered a little. 'But all of the friends stayed nearby down there. I live with my husband, Les.'

'Les Hooper?' he asked. The youngest of the gang. The one Laredo's alcoholic informant back in Flagstaff had described as wanting to be as tough as Asa Taylor and as good with a gun as Harry Speed, but just not having what it took. The girl nodded her agreement. Her smile was tight as she said:

'He is marry me.'

'Why are you up here now; why did you come across the border, Alicia?'

'My husband come with his friends. What else could I do? Besides' — she tossed her head — 'I like it here. I never go hungry, not on this job.'

'You had a hard time of it in Mexico?' Laredo's eyes narrowed. 'But why? I thought your husband and the others were rich men.'

'Some rich!' Alicia leaned back on

the bed, bracing herself with her arms. She fluttered a hand in the air. 'Oh, so Les Hooper wanted a wife and he spoke to my father. He told my father that he was rich and could take care of me — he even showed him a lot of valuable papers.'

Laredo was aching to ask Alicia about those valuable papers, but he decided to let her go on. 'So we have a happy honeymoon in his little house, then we eat nothing but tortillas and beans; that is all there ever was. And guess who makes the tortillas, pat-a-pat, pat-a-pat. It was me.

'The same time Asa and Winslow Pear got the *Federales* after them for stealing horses. They chased them and killed Pear. Asa he made a ride for the border. He has a ranch up here now, in the *Estado Unidos*. He sent a letter not too long ago to my husband and the other men. I remember what it said. 'Time's up, boys. Come on home, I talked to the man not long ago.''

'Cryptic,' Laredo muttered, and

Alicia wrinkled her brow questioningly at the unfamiliar word.

'So we come up here,' she continued, 'not all together. My husband he tells me to try to get a job here. He didn't want me living around that bunch of rough men. Besides, he said, there might be gun trouble before the big pay-off. Like that. That is the way Les Hooper tell me.'

'Was he afraid some of the others might kill him for his share?'

'I don't know. A share of *what*, I don't know. I just know I was a Blue Belle's girl and it was always safe and I always had plenty of good food.'

Laredo paused. There was a lot to mull over in Alicia's story. Could she have made it all up? Not likely, the way she told it quickly and definitely. It seemed that the Red Butte gang — now minus Winslow Pear, killed by the Mexican army — were back and gathered. At Nye's ranch? Or was it Asa Taylor's place? There was a lot to consider.

'But you said you have seen Harry Speed up here,' Laredo prodded. 'In town?'

'Yes, I see him all around,' the girl answered.

Laredo paused, wondering. 'Is he a very pale man who usually wears a black suit?'

Alicia laughed. 'Harry Speed in a town suit? No. And he is not pale — I don't think so, but with his black beard — He started to grow that the day they got to Mexico, Les Hooper tell me. It is a big bushy thing,' she said using her hands to indicate its size.

Laredo nodded. He had not really thought that a gunhand like Harry Speed would hire a local rummy to do his work for him. Unless he had not wanted to draw attention to himself. But Alicia's description of Speed was so different from the man in black Laredo had suspected as to make it ludicrous to believe he was Harry Speed.

Alicia had risen. 'I have to go. They

won't fire me, but I want to stay in good *gracias*.'

'Good graces,' Laredo corrected automatically.

'Oh, so?' Alicia said, cocking her head, digesting that, and smiling.

'Let me give you a little something for your trouble,' Laredo offered, remembering the barely touched money he had withdrawn from the Bisbee bank.

He waited for the regular remarks like 'That's not necessary,' or 'It was no trouble,' but Alicia just waited for her money. Laredo didn't take her for a greedy woman, but as one who felt she had been wrongly deprived so far in life. He gave her five dollars, not knowing if that was too much or too little. No matter, it was slipped into a pocket of Alicia's skirt and then she was gone, leaving Laredo to sit on his bed with the faint, lingering scent of lilac perfume around him, with still more questions that he could not answer. He seemed to accumulate more of these with every day that passed.

He decided to wire Jake Royle in Flagstaff in the morning to see if any new information had reached him. And to let Jake know he was still alive, still on the job.

Laredo rolled up to sleep in the dark comfort of his room. What had he learned? According to Alicia — if she could be trusted, but why not? Where else would she have gotten her information from if she was not Les Hooper's wife, an intimate of the Red Butte gang? No outsider could have known the things she seemed to know, although she might have been shading them for her own purposes.

Then, what had he learned?

Asa Taylor and Winslow Pear had gotten themselves in trouble with the Mexican law for rustling horses. It was no surprise that they had returned to their criminal ways if, as Alicia had told Laredo, they had no money — or none they could convert to ready cash. Only those valuable, useless Series B gold certificates.

All right then, Laredo counted mentally. One, Winslow Pear was no more, having been killed by the Mexican *Federales*. Laredo found himself smiling despite himself. He had never had much of a description of Pear except that the man was said to have three toes missing on his foot. Now, Laredo told himself, at least he wouldn't have to go around tugging the boots off every suspect.

Second, Asa Taylor had come back across the border after the run-in with Mexican law-enforcement and now reputedly had a ranch up here. Was that Randall Nye's place? Was Randall Nye actually Asa Taylor? It seemed possible. For some reason Laredo had never gotten around to getting a description of Nye. Asa Taylor was supposed to weigh over 250 pounds. On a diet of beans and tortillas, Asa might have lost some weight, but at his age men seldom did. His handlebar mustache had no relevance as far as his identity went.

Three, Laredo now had a recent description of Harry Speed, enough to alert him as to who to look out for. There were plenty of men around with large black beards, but Laredo thought Speed would stand out by the way he wore his gun, by his alert eyes. Maybe. But why would Speed want to kill Laredo anyway, not even knowing of his existence?

That was the whole problem here. No one should have known who he was, what his business in Bisbee was, but everyone seemed to suspect or know — something else he would have to ask Jake Royle about. He wished he could talk to the older, more experienced man and get Jake's thoughts on the matter. But that was impossible.

Laredo rolled over and tried to go to sleep as the night rolled by.

The killer burst into his room an hour later.

The door to his room was eased open, but there were enough small warnings to rouse a light sleeper like

Laredo. The small complaint of the hinges on the door, the whisper of boot leather across the floor, the sudden shift in the way the breeze in the room circulated. Laredo shouted out to confuse the intruder, whoever it was, and rolled to the side of the bed, reaching for his Colt in its holster which hung from the bedpost at the head of his bed.

Before he could reach it, a shot was fired into the mattress beside him, a stabbing flame of red light and the scent of burnt black powder following. Laredo was alert enough to squint before the sudden glare of the following shot spewed more blinding light around the room. Finding the familiar walnut grips of his pistol, Laredo continued his roll until he was brought up roughly by the wooden floor. He fired back wildly from his back, hitting nothing but wall, filling the room with still more acrid black smoke.

Someone along the hallway shouted out, and firing his own Colt had assured the intruder that his intended victim still had teeth. The man fled in panic. Laredo did not shoot again.

He rose slowly, the echoes of the gunshots still ringing in his ears. From down the hall more voices joined in a chorus of anger and concern. Hobbling to the door, Laredo saw the hotel desk clerk rushing toward his room. A thin man in a blue town suit, he was bald and just then very agitated. Other guests raised pointing fingers toward Laredo's room. The desk clerk slowed his rush as he neared the scene of violence.

'It's all right now,' Laredo called to him, waving an arm.

'What happened?' The man kept his distance from the armed Laredo.

'Someone tried to kill me in my bed. Did you pass anybody on your way up?'

'No,' the clerk said, stumbling a little over the single word. 'Mister — I'm sorry, but you can't stay here.'

'I'd already reached the same conclusion,' Laredo said drily.

The clerk stood 'tsking' as he looked around the room. Laredo wasted little time dressing and gathering his belongings. At least the little man didn't ask Laredo about paying for the damages. He just stepped aside as Laredo, saddle-bags over his shoulder, rifle and bedroll in his hands, walked out and away.

Laredo met Glen Radcliffe downstairs, pistol in his hand, before he had crossed the hotel lobby.

'You got here fast,' Laredo commented.

'I wasn't far. A citizen came running up to me to say there'd been a shooting at the hotel.'

'There was. At me. I'll tell you about it later.'

Accompanying Laredo across the now deserted lobby, Radcliffe asked, 'Where are you going?'

'I've no idea. Somewhere I can't be found.'

'I've got an empty bunk in the jail if you can stand the occasional noise.'

'I guess I can stand it,' Laredo said, yawning, as they stepped out onto the plankwalk. 'So long as no one's shooting at me.'

'That won't happen. One of my deputies will be there when I'm not.' They stepped down off the walk and continued toward the jail. The night was warm, clear, with a cluster of stars hanging in place above the town.

'Who do you figure did the shooting, Laredo? Not Harry Speed.'

'No, from what I've heard of Speed, it's most unlikely he'd miss hitting a man sleeping in his bed. Besides, the impression I got of this man was that he was clean-shaven.'

Radcliffe didn't understand his meaning so Laredo told him that Alicia had reported Speed was wearing a full dark beard now. Radcliffe nodded, tucking that piece of information away in his mind.

'I don't mind having an idea of what he looks like now so that if I happen to come across him . . . though I haven't got a thing on the man. Any warrant on Speed is long expired by now.'

'Another reason they might have had for lying low in Mexico. But I doubt Speed would be wishing to cause any trouble in Bisbee, and risk getting arrested. He's here for one reason, and one alone: to get his share of the stick-up money.'

'Yeah, well, he's waited long enough for that. Laredo, what makes you think that that's why Speed is in town?'

Laredo told him what he had learned from Alicia and what he deduced from it.

'You think that the whole Red Butte gang, what's left of it, is in Bisbee?' Radcliffe asked as they walked up the steps to his office. Now the sheriff's face was drawn with concern. He wasn't equipped or willing to take on a notorious mob like the Red Butte boys if they decided to make trouble for his town.

'All they want is to finally divide their loot and slip away again,' Laredo told the lawman.

'How do you know?' Radcliffe had halted with his hand on the office doorknob.

'I can't see why they'd stick around otherwise,' Laredo said. 'Alicia thinks that's all they have in mind.'

'Alicia . . . Laredo, you don't think she might have tipped someone to try to kill you?' The sheriff swung the door open.

'No,' Laredo said. 'I really don't, although she might have done so inadvertently. I'm pretty sure I know who did it, and he's had his last chance at me. The next time I see him I'll take him down.'

6

Laredo awoke on a thin cot and wondered for a moment, as he had frequently in his wandering life, where he was and what he was doing there. Oh, yes — the Bisbee jail on one of the sheriff's cots. Thin daylight shone through a high, narrow window. Outside he heard the hum and swarm of bees and the chirping of birds wanting to dine on them. Stretching, he stood up, already dressed down to his boots, as seemed to be his recent habit.

He sat again, waiting for his mind to become fully alert. He knew there were things he needed to do, but could not corral them at the moment. The tempting smell of coffee reached him from up the hall in Radcliffe's office, and he rose, brushing back his hair before he started that way in pursuit of the new day.

'Howdy, Laredo,' Sheriff Radcliffe said from behind his desk. He had his own white mug of coffee in his hand.

'Mind if I share that pot with you?' Laredo asked. As he was pouring himself a cup, he said, 'You look tired this morning, Glen.'

'I am,' Glen Radcliffe admitted. 'Folks catch me napping in the middle of the day and give me a look as if I'm useless. They can't seem to understand that while I work days, most of my clientele is working nights raising hell.'

'I saw a few new guests in the cells. Did you happen to run across anyone we know last night?'

'You mean like Harry Speed, or the man in black? No, I never did, although I was eyeballing every man with a bushy black beard I came across — there are more of them than you'd think.'

'I don't know what it would have profited me if you had,' Laredo said, sagging to a chair. 'You didn't see a man named Stoker or Randall Nye either?'

'Never saw Stoker in my life. I did not see Nye in town: he seldom visits.'

'Stoker is supposed to have a vertical scar across his eye. I don't think you ever did tell me what Nye looks like.'

'Randall Nye,' Radcliffe said, leaning back lazily in his chair. He was fighting a yawn. The one deputy Laredo had met, Earl, entered, not looking pleased with his job on this morning.

'How many, Sheriff?' Earl asked.

'Six new visitors,' Glen answered. 'They're all asleep; no point in asking them if they want breakfast. Just tell them at the restaurant to set up eggs and grits for six.'

'Seems like the county is supporting the Blue Belle,' Earl groused.

'I know, but I'd eat there anyway,' Glen said.

'Well, sure you would . . . ' the deputy began, then thought better of any remark he was about to make. Radcliffe had his eyes briefly closed. He was smiling. Maybe he was stuck on Mabel despite her rather 'meatless' body. None of that was any of Laredo's business.

'You're on telegraph here now, right?' he asked the drowsing lawman.

'Two years now, since those copper miners moved in north of town — those mine bosses have some pull. The office is three blocks up on the right side of the street as you head toward the hotel.'

'Good, I have to wire my boss and tell him what I haven't found and see if he's got anything for me,' Laredo said.

'You were asking about Randall Nye,' Radcliffe said, his eyes still shut.

'Yes, I was.'

'I've been trying to draw up a clear image of the man — I haven't seen him for quite a while, and then only briefly. Something about a permit he needed on his ranch, I can't remember.' Glen Radcliffe gave in to his yawn and released it.

'He's nothing special to look at,' Radcliffe went on. 'A big guy, over two hundred pounds easy. Clean-shaven when I saw him. Only odd thing about him I can think of is his flat face. He looks like he fell face forward into the street and his features just stayed that way forever after.'

'I see,' Laredo said quietly. Where had he seen a man like that lately?

'Does that remind you of someone?' Radcliffe asked. 'You've got a funny look on your face.'

'I often do,' Laredo replied with a lopsided grin. 'I met a man who matches that description out at the Nye ranch. He didn't give a name. But they all swore that Nye wasn't around.'

'They wanted you to go,' Radcliffe said. The sheriff was silent and thoughtful, scratching at his jaw. 'Do you want me to ride out there with you and take a look around?'

'No, I think not, Glen. That badge of yours might spook them, and we don't really want them running off, do we? How would we ever find them again?' Also, it was department policy to never involve local law enforcement in their work if it could be avoided.

Laredo rose, tugging down his hat. 'I think I'd better send my telegram off to Flagstaff — if the office is open this early.'

'I'm pretty sure they are; if not they'll open for you. Tell them I authorized it.' Radcliffe made no attempt to rise and so Laredo crossed to the sheriff's desk and they shook hands. From back in the jail cells the grumbling of the awaking prisoners had begun.

'Another happy day on the farm,' Radcliffe said without a smile.

Laredo grinned and started out. As he walked the street, bright with low morning sunshine, he did a little thinking. How close was he to solving this? Of the six men said to be involved in the Mountain Springs hold-up, only five had been given names so far, but he thought he knew where most were.

Winslow Pear was dead, killed in Mexico for horse-stealing; Harry Speed was walking around in Bisbee, bold as brass, perhaps trusting his beard to hide his features from anyone who might recognize him; that left Asa Taylor, Les Hooper and the man named Stoker. Laredo had come to believe that Randall Nye was actually Asa Taylor. After he had made himself a wanted man in Mexico as well, he had slipped back into the States with or without a small herd of stolen horses which he would have used to start his horse-trading business. He had found himself in need of cash, perhaps to buy land or build structures on his ranch, and tried out of desperation to pass one of the stolen Series B gold certificates at the Bank of Bisbee despite some agreement all the gang had made not to.

Probably he had returned to his old ways and started rustling horses around the territory. Maybe he had made enough money that he was no longer stealing ponies, but actually was a legitimate horse trader, as his reputation had it. It didn't matter for Laredo's purposes.

That cleared up the identities of three of the gang.

The other two, the squat man who resembled a wrestler and the thin one with red hair he had seen at Nye's, must be — almost had to be — Stoker and Alicia's husband, Les Hooper. He had failed to ask her for a description of her husband, and now hesitated to ask. It seemed like a good idea to avoid being seen with Alicia too often.

Hooper was the youngest of the group, and the man with the thin red hair could have been good-looking enough ten years ago. Laredo had noticed at the time that the man deferred to the others, and the constant sneer he wore seemed to have been adopted for the sake of his image. The image of someone who wanted to be as tough as Asa Taylor and as quick with a gun as Harry Speed? He matched the vague descriptions Laredo had of Les Hooper well enough.

Laredo entered the close, musty confines of the telegraph office to find the telegrapher/clerk at his business, transcribing what to Laredo was a series of meaningless clicks being transmitted from somewhere onto a yellow pad, sometimes cocking his head as if that would help him hear the racketing of the key better. Some day, Laredo promised himself, he would take the time to learn Morse code. These telegraphers lived in a mysterious world of their own, speaking their own language.

The clerk glanced up at Laredo, held up a hand gripping a pencil for patience as another staccato burst of clicks sounded, these apparently finishing the message, for the man at the telegraph key answered with a short, magical burst of his own, scribbled down one last hasty note and rose from his desk to meet Laredo.

'Help you?' the man asked. He was narrow with a slightly hawkish nose, wearing a pair of thick-lensed spectacles.

'I need to send a message to Flagstaff — the office of the Bank Examiner's Office there.'

'That's a coincidence,' the man said. 'The message I just got in came from Flagstaff. Your name isn't' — he glanced at his pad — 'Laredo, by any chance?'

'It is.'

'Then this must be for you. It came in as 'Laredo, care of Sheriff Glen Radcliffe'. Let me just write it out in a form you will be able to read — I use a rotten method of shorthand for myself when I'm taking wires.'

Laredo nodded and waited while this was done. He and Jake Royle must have been thinking alike on this morning. Had Jake learned something worth the knowing? He gazed out the clean windows at the passing strangers on the street. He saw Mabel and Alicia arm in arm walking toward the Blue Belle, whispering together and tittering a little as young women will do. He saw no one passing who might have been Harry Speed, nor did he see the man in black. That would have been too much to hope for.

Laredo accepted the telegram from the man. It was terse as most telegrams were. It was from Jake Royle.

NO LUCK, the text read, CANNOT TRACE ANY MEMBER OF THE R.B. GANG. ASSUME STILL IN MEXICO. ONE ITEM: FIFTEEN-YEAR EMPLOY-EE OF FLAGSTAFF BANK, ROGER FRANKLIN, UPPED AND QUIT THE DAY YOU LEFT. REPORT HAS HIM RIDING TOWARD BISBEE. ROYLE.

'Do you want to send an answer?' the telegrapher asked, peering over the top of his glasses.

'Yes. There's no need to write this down,' Laredo said, as the man reached for his pad and pencil. A 'Message received. Laredo' will do it.'

'Saving money?' the telegrapher asked.

'What?'

'It's ten cents a word,' the man said. 'I thought you were maybe trying to save a few cents.'

'No,' Laredo said, smiling as he

fished some change out of his pocket and placed it on the counter. 'That's just all I have to say to the man.'

For the time being.

He had nothing but a handful of assumptions and a couple of wild guesses to share just then, all of which could be wrong. Stepping out into the sunshine of the warming day, Laredo's imagination began working overtime again. Who was Roger Franklin? He fitted in in too many ways to be simple coincidence, but as a part of the puzzle his edges seemed irregular.

Roger Franklin was a town man. He would be wearing a town suit, likely. A black one?

He had left Flagstaff abruptly, shortly after Laredo had. Royle had some word that indicated Franklin was traveling to Bisbee. Where the Red Butte boys happened just now to be holed up in a group. What else did he know about Franklin? He was a banker. And he had been working at the bank when the gold certificates were stolen ten years ago.

If he was the man in black, he had overheard Laredo trying to milk information from the man in the Flagstaff saloon, been concerned enough to warn Laredo and then — concerned enough to quit his job suddenly and follow Laredo to Bisbee?

He would certainly have been able to recognize Laredo and point him out to others: the thugs who had beaten Laredo in the alley for no apparent reason. The Red Butte gang were waiting for something. What? The arrival of the man who had planned the robbery himself — the man who had not been identified by name or description, the sixth member of the gang?

It almost fitted if Laredo considered matters that way, but the pieces did not match smoothly. No matter, he would follow his instincts. He had found his men, thought he was onto their plan, which must involve Roger Franklin, who, perhaps through his banking connections, had found a safe way to cash in the gold certificates now that news of the robbery had cooled down and the money was assumed lost.

That end of things was a little too complicated for Laredo to figure out without consulting with bankers in his own department. Maybe he was wrong about all of it. He didn't think he could be.

Besides, it was the only plan he had to work with and he meant to follow it to the bitter end — which could get really bitter with five Red Butte men around, hungry for the money they had waited ten long years to spend.

Still juggling the fragments of the puzzle, Laredo decided to chance it and go to the kitchen door of the Blue Belle Restaurant and ask Mabel if she knew what Alicia's husband looked like. There was no reason for the waitress to help him out, but he knew that Mabel was more than a little sweet on Glen Radcliffe, and he thought she would do it to shine a little more brightly in the sheriff's eyes.

The sun was riding higher now, sending a sharp glare of yellow light over the false fronts of the buildings along the south side of Main Street. The heat rose as well, and the inevitable dust from the street as horses and wagons passed.

Laredo ducked into a slightly cooler alleyway and made his way to the back door of the restaurant. There was a tantalizing scent of meat roasting within. He wondered how the men and women who worked in the kitchen could stand the summer heat. The door to the kitchen stood wide open of course, and he mounted the three wooden steps to it.

Before Laredo could turn aside, a well-built man with a low-slung Colt and huge, bushy black beard stepped out on the narrow porch of the Blue Belle's kitchen.

7

If Harry Speed recognized him he gave no indication of it. It might have been pretense; there was no way of knowing, but he brushed past Laredo with barely a glance and stepped down into the alley to stride away purposefully.

Laredo watched Speed's back for a few moments then turned toward the kitchen door again. Before he could knock or call out he was met not by Mabel, but by Alicia herself. The slight Mexican girl looked eager, not afraid. She turned Laredo by his shirt front and stepped out onto the porch with him.

'I just saw Harry Speed here. What did he want?'

'Scrambled eggs and toast.'

Laredo sighed inwardly, 'No,' he said, 'I mean, did he come over to talk to you, Alicia?'

'No, why for?' She looked baffled by the question. 'When we first come to Bisbee, Harry Speed say it is not a very good idea for us to have talks. We never speak.'

Laredo hurried on because someone inside the restaurant was calling for Alicia. 'Alicia, what does your husband look like?'

'Les Hooper? Why, you don't want to shoot him, do you?'

'I don't want to shoot anybody,' he assured her.

'Well,' she said doubtfully, as someone again called for her. 'He is tall and narrow. He has red hair, though not so much as he once did,' she admitted with a wry smile. 'Why do you need to know?'

'Alicia!' the voice called for the third time.

She told Laredo, 'They want me to serve. I have to remain in good graces' — she smiled at the term — 'for a little while longer.'

Laredo nodded. He did not want to

get the girl fired. There were no other questions that he could think of to ask anyway, though he wondered as she turned and re-entered the hot kitchen, what had she meant that she had to remain in good graces for a little while longer? Was she planning on leaving Bisbee soon?

It could be, and if so it would fit into the rough timetable Laredo had constructed.

Roger Franklin had arrived. The Red Butte boys had gathered in anticipation of a final pay-off. Maybe Les Hooper had tucked his wife away for the time being and was now planning on having enough ready cash to take her away from Bisbee. Laredo thought that he had better find Franklin and soon, although it was not clear how that would help him recover the stolen gold certificates which was, after all, the whole purpose of his mission.

Where to look for Franklin? The hotel seemed the obvious starting place. Franklin didn't strike him as the sort to camp out in rough country unless forced to.

Walking through a shadowed alley toward the main street once more, he emerged into sunlight to see a familiar face walking swiftly toward Sheriff Radcliffe's office. 'Hello!' Laredo called out, as the telegrapher strode past the alley mouth. The man drew up abruptly, startled.

'Oh, Laredo!' the narrow man said. 'I was just going to the sheriff's office. I have a second wire from Flagstaff for you.' The clerk held up the yellow envelope he was carrying in his scrawny hand and handed it over. Laredo gave him a small tip and watched as the man rushed back toward his office again.

Another telegram from Jake Royle? Laredo tore the envelope open neatly and removed the message.

LAREDO. ROGER FRANKLIN CHIEF TELLER AT BANK FOR FIFTEEN YEARS HAS EMPTIED VAULT OF TEN THOUSAND DOLLARS. HEADED

SOUTH. URGENT KEEP EYES OPEN
FOR HIM. ROYLE.

Laredo read it twice although there
was no need to. He thought that the
wire cleared things up a little as far as
Franklin's dealings went. The Red
Butte boys had $50,000 in stolen gold
certificates that they could not convert
to hard cash. Franklin thought he
could, but he would have to show some
earnest money to Asa Taylor and the
others to convince them to turn the
bonds over to him. The $10,000 could
be represented as good-faith money
with the rest to come later through
Franklin's banking contacts. Whether
Franklin intended to follow through
with the deal was a question that not
only occurred to Laredo but certainly
would to the experienced thieves in the
Red Butte gang. They would never
agree to accept twenty cents on the
dollar for the bonds, not after ten years
of waiting for the pay-off.

If Franklin, the inexperienced banker

recently turned thief himself, figured he could outwit the old-time criminals, he was not only flirting with disaster, he was nearly wed to it. Laredo strode across the street and down it toward the stable.

It seemed certain that there would be a meeting now, and the site had to be the 'Nye ranch'. There was no way that the entire Red Butte gang would come traipsing into Bisbee to meet in, say, Franklin's hotel room. That would destroy the cloak of anonymity they had been working to weave.

No, they would hold the meeting at the ranch — and soon. Roger Franklin was now on the run himself. Laredo's thoughts flickered back to the sight of Harry Speed slipping out the back door of the Blue Belle Restaurant. Had he gone there to give Alicia the message that the gang was preparing to move on? That her husband would soon have gotten paid, and to be ready to go?

No way of knowing. If it was so, Alicia was a better liar than Laredo had taken her for. But he had been tricked by good liars before. A waitress who earned her money for tips by smiling at all her customers could learn well to sham. Laredo shook his head — Alicia was the least of his concerns.

Asking, as he saddled his gray in the darkened mustiness of the stable, Laredo learned that a man had come in not an hour earlier to hire a buggy. He was not a local man, but he was well dressed and seemed to have enough money to lend him credence as a good risk. A wealthy horse buyer, the stable-hand took him for. He had enquired about the way to Randall Nye's ranch.

Laredo paid for his horse's boarding and hit the long trail east, hurrying the gray along. Could he catch Franklin before he reached the Nye ranch? Although the money involved wasn't as great as that the Red Butte gang had taken at Mountain Springs, Franklin was every bit as much of a thief — and the sort the banks detested: a trusted man who steals from his own. Laredo wanted badly to catch the man.

True, law enforcement across the territory would soon be notified to be on the lookout for Franklin, but Laredo was riding now practically in his shadow. He had thought of enlisting Radcliffe in this pursuit, but that would have taken a lot of explaining and planning time. Besides, his agency had always prided itself on working alone — unwisely at times, Laredo reflected.

It didn't matter now. The decision, however hasty, had been made.

It might have been made too hastily. Peering ahead constantly as he tried to locate the man he believed to be Franklin, Laredo had inexcusably been neglecting his back trail. Now, as he glanced back, he saw the rider there. He was not coming fast, but he was coming. The man knew the country, there was no doubt of that, for he stayed within the thin border of the scattered trees, shielding himself from clear observation.

Harry Speed? Laredo could not be sure at this distance, but he thought it might be the gunman with the huge black beard. Speed, after all, had been in Bisbee. He could have seen the telegrapher and Laredo meet. Alicia could have let something slip, or have deliberately informed Speed, if she thought that Laredo was a threat to the new-found freedom which Les Hooper's share of the stolen money could purchase for her.

Alicia had seemed to be content working in the Blue Belle, but what woman would wish to work forever serving platters in a hot restaurant when her husband had the money to take her away to live anywhere she might choose?

Laredo felt that he must be slipping as he realized he had picked up a pursuer. Too old for this sort of trail, maybe? He had considered quitting before, after a few bloody encounters, and settling down finally with Dusty, who had all the money they would ever need, maybe moving to Flagstaff and sitting in a comfy office all day like Jake Royle, who had similarly tired of tracking outlaws for a living. It was no time for daydreaming about these things now. They would do nothing to extricate him from the mess he had gotten himself into at the present.

The plan was . . . what was the plan? He couldn't just follow Franklin onto the Nye property and demand that everyone hand over their stolen property. He couldn't threaten them or outgun them. The men in the Red Butte gang had been playing with guns for a long time, and their play was quite deadly. In the house, Laredo now knew, were Asa Taylor, Stoker and Les Hooper. On the trail behind him was Harry Speed. It was not what you'd call a good situation.

Laredo briefly regretted not bringing some help. But what help could Sheriff Radcliffe and a bunch of deputies be? Approaching the house with such an army would lead to a savage battle, a bloody stand-off. Or, alternatively, a humiliating retreat for the law. Glen Radcliffe had no reason to arrest any of the men there — with the exception of Roger Franklin, for whom he had probably not received a warrant as of yet, the bank theft being so recent. Nye — Asa Taylor — could just laugh the sheriff off the property.

No, as much as he regretted it Laredo would have to play his hand alone as he had in the past. He heeled the gray slightly, asking it for more speed. He still wanted to catch up with Roger Franklin before he could reach the ranch, if possible. Even if he succeeded, Laredo had no real idea of what to do after that.

And he had Harry Speed riding in his tracks. Some days . . . and this was one of them.

Laredo spotted a man in a buggy ahead of him; the gray's increased pace had brought him up on the coat-tails of the fleeing bank teller. He urged the horse on still more. He was riding in the dust cloud the buggy wheels threw up now, the gray running steadily, swiftly on. Laredo saw a pale face look back at him from the buggy, saw the sun glint off the muzzle of a small-bore handgun. Was the man in black going to make a fight of it? It seemed so, unaccustomed as he must have been to gunplay.

Well, desperate men adopt desperate measures. Roger Franklin had everything to lose if he were stopped now, short of his goal. Firing across his shoulder from a moving, bouncing buggy was not his best choice, but it was his only choice if he were to survive. A gun sang out before Laredo had even drawn his own weapon and he felt the impact and fiery pain of a bullet slamming into his body, high on the shoulder. Laredo was shocked and sent tumbling from the saddle by the heavy bullet which had not been fired from Franklin's gun, but from a rifle behind Laredo.

Harry Speed had made the first play

in the game, and he had made it a good one.

* * *

What time was it? Where was he and what was he doing there? The sun was lower in the western sky, which meant it was approaching evening where he lay at the bottom of a brushy ravine, its flanks studded with nopal cactus and dense with purple sage.

His shoulder was gripped with sudden savage pain as he was jerked into rough consciousness and very nearly dropped back into the dark abyss of oblivion again. He could not allow that to happen.

Laredo had lost hours, and only by the slimmest whim of fate not his life. He clawed himself to a sitting position on the rock-strewn earth. A faint breeze whispered down the shallow ravine. An alligator lizard looked at him with goggling eyes and then scurried away. A living man was of no interest to him.

The red ants swarming over his legs and arms did not discern the difference. Laredo brushed them away with angry swipes of his good hand. His left hand, he had discovered on his first attempt at movement, tingled, was nearly paralyzed, practically useless.

As was Laredo.

He doubted he could ride even if he knew where his horse was. The way his head swam and spun made him doubt his ability to use a gun even if closely threatened. He did retain his Colt .44 revolver, slung in his battered holster, but he glanced down at it only as a sort of curiosity, not as a tool of his trade.

He heard a horse whicker not far away. He thought it was his gray, but had no way of being sure. He tried whistling it up, more softly than he would usually have, for there was no telling what ears were about. He considered the possibility that Harry Speed had waited around to be sure of his kill, but then Speed would have been more likely to accompany Roger

Franklin to the Nye ranch now that he believed the long-awaited payday was at hand. What did he care about Laredo, so long as he was out of the game?

Laredo heard a stirring in the brush along the ravine, and he reached for his pistol with an instinct ingrained by leading a life of trouble. His eyes shifted eastward, away from the sun. He heard faintly the clicking of steel-shod hoofs moving over the stones in the gully bottom.

The squarish head of his stolid gray horse appeared, peering over the screen of brush which partially hid Laredo from view. Laredo whistled again, and the horse now moved toward him without caution. Reaching him, the horse dropped its muzzle and Laredo stroked it.

'I am very glad to see you,' Laredo whispered to the animal, brushing away a deer fly from the horse's eye as he spoke. Then came the hard part. How was he going to get in the saddle with one arm practically useless, stunned and bleeding? *Through grit*, he told himself angrily. He had been in worse positions, though just then he couldn't remember when.

Turning, Laredo managed to leverage himself to a kneeling position. His patient horse remained in place, though it did crane its neck to give its master a puzzled look. Laredo took hold of the stirrup and lifted himself up. He still did not dare try to use his left arm. He could now feel warm blood still trickling from the fresh bullet wound. The loss of blood brought with it a dizziness. Laredo stood, head against his saddle, eyes closed, waiting for the dizzy spell to pass — if it would.

Poking his left foot into the stirrup, he used his right hand to try to drag himself up into leather. He was almost amazed when he made it instead of ending up face down on the ground below. Reaching around the horse's neck he managed to snatch up his reins. He sat breathing hard, vision blurred, shoulder throbbing. Laredo knew that having made it that far he ought to turn the horse's head toward Bisbee and seek medical help: it was the only sane thing to do.

Laredo headed the horse down the gully and they climbed a shallow slope to emerge on the flats above the Nye ranch, where . . . Well, who knew what had transpired there in the past few hours? Laredo still felt that he could bring a successful end to this, a confidence based on nothing but blind faith — ignorance, some might have said, and they would probably be right.

Yet Laredo had been too successful for too long in so many episodes that he had poisoned his own mind, or so it seemed. Dusty always scolded him, but not for long, when he dragged himself home, sometimes needing months of rest before he was fit for the road again. And the woman was absolutely right. But then, she was smarter than he was.

Maybe he would need no scolding this time; maybe this time he would not make it home.

As he sat on the ridge contemplating his options, which were fewer than they had been before he was wounded, his decision was made for him. Bursting out of the valley which surrounded the Nye ranch came a black buggy. The man driving it was whipping his bay horse unmercifully, his eyes wide as he raced toward some goal or away from some demon.

It was Roger Franklin, and he was driving as if fleeing a forest fire.

The buggy emerged on the flatlands and turned southward. Laredo saw no following pursuit from the Nye ranch, which caused everything to seem odd, wrong somehow. If the Red Butte gang was after him, there would have been activity down on the ranch. If they were not, Franklin was driving like a madman for no particular reason. Laredo sloughed off the questions for the time being. With one last glance at the ranch he fell in behind Roger Franklin. That horse and buggy were not going to run that fast for long, they were not capable of it, and so Laredo did not hurry his gray excessively.

He needed to catch Franklin. He was the one who knew what had happened at the ranch, what the entire plan had been. On top of that Franklin had pulled another bank job in Flagstaff, and that made it Laredo's business.

Oh, yes, that bay horse would slow, the buggy would have to halt. Laredo, wounded, would be slowed as well. But he would not be stopped, as Roger Franklin should have realized by now.

8

The bay horse drawing Roger Franklin's buggy faltered, stumbled and seemed on the verge of foundering. Laredo felt no better than that poor, abused animal; he was still leaking blood, but the gray horse he rode was strong and confident. He managed to catch up with the buggy at the verge of the scattered pine forest. The trees growing there all looked yellowed and bedraggled. The man guiding the bay horse looked no better.

Dust drifted past them as Laredo grabbed the bay's halter, and turned, gun drawn to face Roger Franklin one more time.

'Don't shoot me,' an exhausted voice said. 'I've had enough.'

A woman's face appeared: she had been hiding against the buggy's floor. 'I always pick the weak men!' Alicia said with disgust.

'What is she doing here?' Laredo had to ask, although he thought he knew — at least partially.

'She pleaded with me. Jumped on the buggy as I was making my escape,' Franklin said, mopping the perspiration from his red face. The man was obviously out of his sphere, dealing with men too tough and savage for him. Laredo could have told him that beforehand.

Patiently, as much for himself as for the others, including the frothing, shuddering bay horse, he invited them to step down, not lowering his Colt. The man in the black suit looked behind, watching for any pursuit. He was deeply frightened, no doubt of that. Alicia leaped down from the carriage spryly. Although her face reflected anger, she seemed to be treating this as a game. She now wore a pair of blue jeans and a flowered shirt in place of her yellow waitress dress.

'Well, now you can shoot them all, I don't care,' Alicia said to Laredo, waving her hands in the air.

Roger Franklin had staggered from the buggy to the shade of a gnarled, dusty pine where he seated himself on the ground. Laredo, more weary than Franklin was, joined him there. A faint breeze shifted the upper reaches of the pine. Alicia plopped down not far from the men. Laredo continued to stand over Franklin, his Colt now holstered. A scolding crow circled briefly and then disappeared. The bay horse continued to stand quivering. Laredo's gray nuzzled it once and then began a search for forage.

'You like to kill that horse,' Laredo said. Franklin glanced up at him and nodded.

'I know it, and I'm sorry for the animal, but we were running for our lives.'

'No one's pursuing you,' Laredo told him.

'No. I see that — now. But when a

bunch of tough armed men tell you to get going, you get going!'

'I thought you were their friend,' Laredo said.

'Thieves, cut-throats! Do men like that have friends?'

'Not as a general rule,' Laredo replied. His shoulder was fiery, sore. Too bad about that here and now.

He asked Franklin, 'What happened back there? What went wrong with your plan?'

'Only everything,' the man in black told him, closing his eyes briefly. Alicia had wandered back toward the buggy. Laredo watched her closely, but she only went to the bay horse and stroked it, her eyes on some distant goal. Franklin flicked idly at some of the dust coating his trousers.

'I had a deal for them, but Asa Taylor was having none of it. He said they'd waited long enough for me to come through.'

'You offered them the ten thousand dollars.'

'Yes,' Franklin said, surprised that Laredo knew about that stolen money. He shrugged as if it didn't matter any more, which it didn't. 'I told them it would take me only a few days more to exchange the gold certificates. I knew now how to do it. There's a man — a moneylender and sometime swindler in Denver who would be happy to take the whole batch. I knew he wouldn't dare back out if I showed up with the Red Butte boys at my shoulder.'

'That wasn't good enough for Asa?'

'No, although I was willing to give him ten thousand as good-faith money.'

'He took that, I assume. And then you had already been careless enough to give Taylor the name of the man in Denver who would deal in stolen gold certificates.'

Franklin nodded. 'Plain stupid, wasn't I?'

'You've been acting stupid for quite a while now,' Laredo said without sympathy.

'Yes, maybe. But there was no going

back on the deal once it was made. You can't go back on Asa Taylor and live. That's why I brought the ten thousand with me. I thought if they saw the cash, they'd realize that I was sincere about the rest of the bargain.'

'You're the one who informed them of the gold certificates in the first place, aren't you?' Laredo asked, already knowing the answer.

'Yes. I met Taylor and Winslow Pear at the saloon in Flagstaff one night. They started bragging about some of the robberies they had pulled. I told them more than I should have about the arriving gold certificates, coming on a stagecoach with only the driver. It seemed a way to make myself fit in with the rough crowd.'

'So they thought they'd found a sucker, used what you told them to hold up the stage at Mountain Springs and made off with the gold certificates. When did it all break down, Franklin?'

'Almost immediately. I told them that the certificates were brand new and that the serial numbers were known. They could not be passed through any normal channels. Asa Taylor hit the roof. He asked if I thought they had gone through that for nothing. I told him to take it easy, the heat was bound to cool down. I think I was the one who suggested they go down to Mexico and hole up for a while. Anyway, that's what they did.

'None of them liked it particularly, not without money to spend. I guess Asa and Winslow Pear — maybe some of the others — started raising a ruckus down there.'

'Horse-stealing,' Laredo said.

'Among other things, it seems. Anyway, they had hardly forgotten about me. Recently, I wrote them and told him that they could come back, I had things in hand. Asa, I later found out, was already here.'

'As Randall Nye.'

Franklin gave Laredo an odd look, perhaps wondering where he had come by his information.

'But then the contact I thought I had was arrested for trying to short-deal the army on a supply contract, and I was really in it. How could I tell Asa that my deal had fallen apart, that after ten years I had nothing to show them?'

A few flies had discovered them and swarmed around noisily. They seemed especially interested in Laredo's wounded shoulder. Blood still seeped through his shirt and he was getting sleepy, too sleepy listening to Franklin. He wished the man would hurry up. He saw Alicia strolling a little way off as if she were out looking for wildflowers.

'You panicked,' he suggested to Franklin.

'Yes. I had come across a new money man in Colorado, but he was not about to advance me anything on my word alone. He told me it was pay on delivery, which I understand, but what was I going to tell Asa? I had suggested to him that I had cash money ready for him. That lie . . . ' Franklin admitted hesitantly, 'I told him out of plain fear.'

'So you robbed your own bank.' Laredo shook his head. 'One more stupid idea.'

'It was that or have the Red Butte boys kill me! I thought if I could give them enough money to assure them . . . That didn't work.'

'It's amazing how far your greed has pushed you,' Laredo commented without emphasis.

'You wouldn't believe how little the bank was paying me!' Franklin said, his face flushing with indignation. 'I would be promised raises, even a partnership, and then forgotten when the time came.'

'You made more than most working men do. You think the average cowboy has it easier than you did?' Laredo asked with some bitterness. He went on, 'No, you got yourself into this because of greed, maybe because of the need to be a big man in front of the Red Butte boys. You can't play games with men like that, Franklin. They have a different set of rules. Now, tell me what happened back at the ranch.'

Alicia was wandering toward them, her hands behind her back, scuffing her boots along as she approached.

'Just what you'd think,' Franklin said, lifting his eyes briefly to watch the girl. 'Asa asked me to hand over the money, then laughed and said it wasn't even half enough. Without thinking I told him about the buyer I had in Denver. He said, fine, that's where he would take the gold certificates.

'When I asked him for some of the money back for my share, Taylor just laughed. Harry Speed was there, and he laughed too — for a moment. Then he told Asa that they couldn't simply let me go now that I knew what their plan was. I believe that they were only trying to scare me. And it worked.

'I half-convinced them that I couldn't go to the authorities now since I had just robbed the Bank of Flagstaff and anyway was complicit in the Mountain Springs hold-up. Which is true,' Franklin added after a breath.

'What about her?' Laredo asked, lifting his chin toward Alicia. 'How did she come to be with you?'

'I told you how,' Franklin said. 'She just jumped into the buggy as I was leaving. As to why — you'd have to ask her.'

He watched as Alicia sauntered toward them, arms swinging freely. She smiled at him. The smile showed a lot of teeth, but little pleasure. She squatted down comfortably beside him.

'Alicia,' Laredo asked, 'what are you doing here?'

She looked down as she spoke, sifting dirt through her fingers. 'The Harry Speed, he came by to tell me that it was time to collect their money.'

'I figured as much.'

'So I rushed out, changed my clothes and rode to meet my husband. He seemed glad to see me — at first. Later, after all the men had finished the bargaining and Asa Taylor had yelled a lot at this man' — she nodded at Roger Franklin — 'Les was counting some

142

money and I leaned over his shoulder.

' 'Now we can live decent,' I told him.

' 'I don't think so,' was what he said to me. He told me that it had been all right with me while he needed me, but now he had money and they were riding to get more, he didn't want me hanging around.

'He said I had a good job and a place to stay, and was better off than I had been in Mexico. I would be just sucking money off of him now if he let me. But he wasn't going to let me.

'I argued; he argued. He told me what a stupid woman I was. It got crazy enough that he pulled his gun and said he'd shoot me if I didn't get out of there and leave him alone. I believed him. The others just watched.'

'What did they say?' Laredo asked.

'They don't say nothing. It was between a man and his wife. They don't want to hear it. Asa, he was already mad himself. He and Harry Speed waved guns at this man, and he ran out.'

'I did,' Franklin said. 'I'm not proud of it, but I did. They looked like they were all mad enough to kill.'

'I see this man starting his buggy and I run and jump onto it. I didn't know if Les Hooper was going to kill me then. We drove off, very fast, and the last thing I heard was all of the men laughing. Les was laughing too.'

'He wouldn't have killed you,' Laredo believed.

'Maybe no,' Alicia said, shrugging her thin shoulders. 'But he was not going to take me with him.' Her words stuttered to a stop. 'He had wounded my pride. Maybe I would have followed along and killed him.'

'Now what, Alicia?'

She shook her head slowly. 'I don't know what now. I think I go back to the Blue Belle — maybe not.'

'What about you, Franklin?' Laredo asked.

'Do I have a choice? Aren't you arresting me?'

'I don't have the authority to do that.

I'm only after the money. Local lawmen, eventually even bounty hunters, will be on your trail before long, though. And they'll catch you.

'The best thing you could do,' Laredo advised the banker, 'is to go back into Bisbee and turn yourself in to the sheriff, Glen Radcliffe, because I'm sorry, but a man like you out here trying to run from the law just won't last long. You haven't got a chance.'

After a thoughtful moment, Franklin said, 'I suppose not.'

'Your horse has had a good long rest. He's probably fit enough to get you back to Bisbee if you walk him.'

'I don't see that I have any other choice,' Franklin said, rising to his feet. 'It's all over.'

Alicia asked Laredo, 'What about you, Laredo? Where will you be going? Is it over for you too?'

'No, it isn't. For me it's just beginning.'

'How can you say so?' she said. 'You are going after four very bad men to try to take the money from them? Laredo, don't you know that this is impossible?'

'Yeah,' he muttered, 'I know. That's what I tried to tell my boss.'

He watched as Franklin stepped into the buggy, followed by Alicia, who had no choice but to go along. 'Give me your coat,' Laredo said to Franklin.

'What?'

'I said give me your coat. I want it.'

Franklin, puzzled, complied, shrugging out of his black coat and handing it to Laredo. Then he started the bay horse, very slowly, and turned it around toward Bisbee. It took Laredo a little time and some pain to shoulder into the coat, which wasn't a bad fit. It was still warm at this time of day, but Laredo hadn't wanted it for its protection from the cold. He needed it to cover his wounded shoulder. It might not help if he happened to meet Harry Speed, but then, Speed had never seen him close up except for the brief moments on the Blue Belle's porch, and Speed was showing no interest then.

Laredo managed to get into the saddle again and he started the gray horse toward the Nye ranch, for he did not believe that Asa Taylor would be in a big rush to leave although the others might be. Asa Taylor had a few dozen head of good horses on the ranch, and he would not simply ride off and leave them behind. He had too much invested in them. Could he drive them all the way to Colorado? What would be the point in that? He would be willing to sell them quickly and at a good price. That, of course, required a buyer. Who better than the man who had already shown an interest in his herd — Laredo?

At least that was Laredo's thinking as he again wound his way down the long trail toward the ranch. Too much could go wrong, he knew. Starting with Harry Speed, who might recognize Laredo as the man he had shot and left for dead. It was Laredo's horse especially that Speed might recognize, for Laredo's features at 200 yards would have been indistinct. Then, too, Asa Taylor might be tired of the 'horse buyer' he had ordered off his property earlier, but Laredo thought not.

At that time the gang had still been waiting, watching for Roger Franklin to arrive with their money. And probably discussing how they were going to kill Franklin and keep the money they thought he was bringing and the gold certificates as well.

The banker should have known that he was never going to get out of there having made a profit, but Franklin was in too deep and he was desperate. For now Laredo's only chance was to act utterly ignorant and pursue the purchase of a few horses. Asa might decide that Laredo should not be allowed to ride off, but then why would he do that? He would have Laredo's money and would have gotten rid of a few of the horses which were of no use to him anyway.

It was still light when Laredo rode into the yard of the ranch although it was not long until dusk would settle. Laredo's eyes flickered around the yard, looked at the face of the house. No one could be seen moving. Maybe, Laredo thought, he had guessed wrong and Asa Taylor had struck out for richer lands, leaving his horse herd behind.

But he had not.

'Hold it right there and get down off that horse,' a voice called out, and Laredo complied. 'Now walk slowly up to the house!'

Laredo did so and started toward the front door of the ranch house for what he knew could very well be the last time one way or another.

9

The stubby man he now knew to be the outlaw, Stoker, guided him with his rifle barrel up onto the porch. Laredo tried to look bewildered.

'Is Nye home now?' he asked Stoker, who grunted something that wasn't meant to be a response.

'This is the oddest outfit,' Laredo tried. 'Have you boys some sort of trouble?'

'Comin' in!' Stoker called out and with his rifle motioned for Laredo to enter the house.

He knew the men inside. Asa Taylor sat in a wooden chair beside the cold fireplace, Les Hooper glanced at him from the corner, perhaps still holding a grudge over his last meeting with Laredo when he had taken a strongly thrown elbow in his gut. Harry Speed sat on the sofa, his eyes dark and brooding.

'So you came back,' Asa said with the faintest of smiles.

'I still wanted to talk to Randall Nye. You'd be surprised how scarce good horses are in this part of the country.'

'Wait a minute,' Harry Speed said, 'I've seen this man before. He was in Bisbee.'

'We've all seen him before,' Asa Taylor said. 'His name is Larry Cotton and he rode out here looking to buy some of Randall Nye's horses earlier. As for being in Bisbee, where else would you expect him to be? Where did you see him?'

'At the Blue Belle Restaurant,' said Harry Speed, stroking his heavy beard. Laredo continued to try to look confused, innocent.

'A man going to eat. Quite suspicious,' Asa said, with a hint of mockery in his voice. It was obvious who was in charge here.

'Stoker, get back to standing lookout, just in case. Take the kid with you.' Les Hooper's mouth opened as if he would like to say something, probably about being called 'kid' at his age, but he shut it again without forming any words.

Harry Speed, on his feet now, went to the window at the front of the house and looked out as Stoker and Les Hooper got their gear together to return to the lookout post. Stoker had a wary look in his beady little eyes as if he did not like being away from where the money was kept. It was likely. Were Asa Taylor and Speed capable of double-crossing their associates of so many years and running off with the loot? Laredo thought probably so, and Stoker seemed to have his qualms about being sent away from the house again.

Each of them had suffered for the past ten years, waiting for their share of the Mountain Springs money and Laredo thought he could sense the mistrust among them. Harry Speed had parted the curtains and was looking out into the front yard.

'I know that horse this man is riding. I saw it not a couple of hours ago,'

Harry Speed said. 'He was following you-know-who in his buggy. I picked him off.'

'You shot me! But why?' Laredo exclaimed.

Asa motioned for Speed to calm down. To Laredo he said, 'Why don't you tell me about it.'

Laredo said, 'I decided to give Randall Nye one more chance before I rode out of this country having accomplished nothing. I saw someone driving a buggy this way. I thought it might be Nye, so I tried to catch up with him. Then I was shot out of my saddle.'

Asa gave Harry Speed a look which was not at all complimentary.

'You weren't wearing no coat then,' Harry Speed said irrelevantly.

'Why, no. It's growing cool out. I had the coat in my saddle-bags.' Laredo continued to try to look bewildered. Asa turned Speed by his shoulder and turned him away after whispering a few words to the bearded gunman. Harry Speed shuffled off unhappily toward the back of the house. Laredo soon discovered that Asa was trying to calm things down. Every one of the Red Butte boys was jittery. Asa adopted the stance of a reasonable man.

'We've had some trouble around here lately; my boys are a little on edge. By the way, if you haven't guessed, my name is Randall Nye.'

'I hadn't,' Laredo lied, thrusting out a hand to the flat-faced man. 'I'm glad to meet you. Maybe we can finally get down to talking about what brought me here — horses.'

'Maybe we can, Mr Cotton. In fact I think we should.' Asa Taylor sat down on his wooden chair again and offered a seat to Laredo. 'This is not the way gentlemen conduct business, but I was wondering, could you show me some bona fides in the form of cash money? You see, we have had a few would-be swindlers around lately.'

Laredo tried to look shocked. He produced the $200 he had drawn from the Bank of Bisbee and apologized.

'The rest of my roll is in the bank in town. I didn't think it was safe to wander around with so much money.'

'No. Quite wise of you,' Asa said, as if he understood the wickedness of men all too well. 'How many horses were you looking for?'

'That depends on what you have to show me. Perhaps only five or six, perhaps all you have save the infirm.'

Asa Taylor said with some pride, 'I have no infirm animals in my string.'

'I'd have to look them over, of course, and unfortunately . . . ' Laredo motioned toward the window where settling dusk was evident. It was already dark enough in the room to make a lantern welcome. 'That will have to wait until morning, Mr Nye. After I've examined the ponies, perhaps you and I can ride into Bisbee and close the deal at the bank.'

'That might be all right,' Asa Taylor said. Harry Speed hung back in the heavy shadows. Obviously he had been listening.

'Of course, I'll have to hire some men on to help me drive them north. If all goes well, we can have everything finished by afternoon. Mr Nye? Are you quitting the horse-trading business?' Laredo asked innocently.

'I've got a little family trouble up in Colorado that I have to take care of,' Nye said, rising. Without saying a word to 'Larry Cotton', the outlaw swept up the $200 as if they had done their deal and he was accepting the down payment.

Laredo stood, not making a comment. The money, he noticed, went not into Taylor's billfold but into a small black leather satchel in the closet.

'Well, it's a long ride back to Bisbee,' Laredo said, rising to stretch. 'I'd better get started before full dark.'

'That's a long way to go, down and back. Stay here. You can look over the horses first thing in the morning, then I'll go with you into Bisbee to finish the bank business. In twenty-four hours we'll both be satisfied men.'

'All right,' Laredo said, searching for the right reaction. 'Larry Cotton' wouldn't have found any objection to the plan, but then again Larry Cotton wouldn't have known that he was being invited to sleep in an outlaw stronghold where any mistake could cost him his life. 'That sounds like as good a plan as any.'

Asa then led Laredo to a room which was no larger than a cell and probably was intended to act as one. There was a bed, a table and a window so small that a pygmy couldn't have wriggled through it. There was a lantern on the table; Asa flicked a match to life and lit it before departing, wearing his benevolent horse-trader's smile.

Well, Laredo thought, looking around the small, drab room, he had gotten himself inside the gang. Whether he could get himself out again was a different problem. Laredo thought that he could. Asa Taylor needed to sell those horses, and Laredo was here, now. Taylor wanted to get to the bank in the morning and make a few thousand dollars more which he would not have to share with his gang. If something went wrong in Colorado, Asa would still have something in his purse to start over. To draw money from the bank, Asa needed Larry Cotton and he needed him alive.

Laredo did not remove his boots or his gun. At the sounds of muted conversation beyond the walls to his room he went to press his ear against the door. The two men were still in the living room: Asa Taylor and Harry Speed. He knew them by their voices, but could not make out all of the words they spoke.

' . . . But why?' Harry Speed was asking.

'We are . . . a business deal, and he's the money man. I can't ride off and lose the investment I have in — '

'I don't like it . . . don't know for sure who he is. If he's gotten wise to us — ' Speed objected.

'Another reason to keep him here,

Harry. He can't tell anyone so long as — '

The men talked on, but there was no point in eavesdropping any longer. Speed didn't like Laredo being in the house, but Asa Taylor would win the discussion. He was, after all, the leader of the Red Butte boys, and he was the one holding the gang's money. He was more of a planner than the quick-to-the-gun Harry Speed. The other two men were still standing guard in the night, which would grow chill soon enough.

Who would relieve them? Speed, of course. Asa Taylor would not leave the house and the money. Laredo sat on the edge of his bed, pondering. What he needed now was some way to divide the gang or at least pare them down. With no plan of action, he went out of the room to find Asa and Harry Speed still in the living room. Asa was smoking a thin cigar. Smoke wreathed his flat face and square head. The eyes of both men flickered toward him.

'I need to put up my horse. Can't have him standing where he is all night.'

'All right,' Asa Taylor said, with the understanding smile of another man who cared for horses. 'Harry here will show you where to put it.'

Grumbling, Harry Speed rose. 'Come along, Cotton,' he growled from behind his black beard. 'I have to get going anyway.' He shot Asa a murderous glance which indicated that things were not at all right between the two. 'I've got to stand guard duty.' Speed picked up his rifle which was standing beside the doorway, snatched up his coat, and opened the door to the clear, cold night.

The two outlaws seemed on the verge of a falling-out, and Laredo thought he could understand why.

Speed had continued living in near-poverty in Mexico while Asa Taylor had returned north and started a profitable horse ranch. More, Asa Taylor had control of the gang's money and he meant to keep it. If it were up to Speed, obviously the gang would be off now, riding toward Colorado and the money dealer to exchange the gold certificates. In Speed's eyes Asa was dawdling over a few horses and the chance to take Larry Cotton for a few more dollars, of which Speed would receive no share.

'Come on,' Speed said, separating himself from Laredo a little and walking at his side instead of leading the way. Harry Speed obviously still did not trust his presence. Laredo untied his gray and led it along. Speed gestured with his rifle to the right of the house and Laredo walked that way leading his horse. They came upon a ramshackle barn not much larger than a tool shed. It was the only structure Laredo had seen on the ranch that wasn't well constructed. Perhaps a barn had seemed unimportant to Asa Taylor, or maybe by the time he got around to it he already knew that the life of the 'Nye ranch' was nearly at an end.

'About time!' a voice growled at them from out of the darkness. It was the thick, squat Stoker who had called out. 'It's getting damned cold up there; I didn't even have a coat with me. I told the kid that I was coming in and the hell with Asa.'

'You'd waited a few more minutes and I'd've been there,' Harry Speed told him.

'And how was I supposed to know that? Remember that day at Black Rock when — '

Speed cut off the old complaint. 'Just watch this *hombre* while he puts his horse up. Then take him back to the house. You can tell Asa your problems — though I doubt he'll listen.'

Harry Speed swung into the saddle of his roan which had stood there outfitted since he had ridden in. It was the outlaw way, Laredo knew. Always have your horse ready to ride, because you never know.

Laredo turned to watch Harry Speed ride away. It was Stoker's turn to growl at him. 'See to your horse, will you? I haven't even got a coat on. Blamed foolish business standing guard over something we could just have ridden away with.'

'You were wishing to take the horse herd on a night drive?' Laredo asked innocently. Briefly Stoker looked at him as if Laredo were the stupidest man alive, then remembered the horse buyer was supposed to know nothing of the money. Laredo had unfastened his cinches. Now he stopped and looked at Stoker, whose mind was elsewhere.

'How about a hand? I don't know if I can move my saddle. Your friend, Mr Speed, put a bullet through my shoulder.'

'He did, did he? Must've had a reason for doing so.'

'Not that he ever explained,' Laredo said. Obviously Stoker was not used to doing another man's work for him, but, grumbling, he came forward, muttering.

'Anything that'll get me out of here and into a warm house. Sittin' on a hill, this time of night, listening to that dumb Les Hooper tell his stories. The only thing even halfway interesting about the kid is his wife! And the dumb bastard chased her off — '

That was as far as Stoker got with his complaints. As he hoisted the saddle from the back of Laredo's gray horse and turned his back, Laredo stepped forward and clubbed the man down with a solid blow of his Colt's barrel thudding against bone just over Stoker's ear. Stoker dropped Laredo's saddle, then he himself dropped to the ground, out cold.

One down, Laredo told himself as he stood over the unconscious Stoker. He was down, although what good that would do Laredo in the long run, he could not be sure.

For now he and Asa Taylor were the only two men on the ranch. If he could get the drop on Asa and recover the money . . . no, that was no good. He would never make it back to Bisbee alive. Not with two sentries posted. He did not know the country around well enough to devise another escape route — besides in the darkness, it would probably prove futile. Better to stick with the original plan, such as it was.

If Asa Taylor was convinced to ride to the bank at Bisbee with Laredo, would he leave the gold certificates behind? Highly unlikely. He trusted his associates no more than they trusted him.

That meant that Laredo would have Asa alone on the trail with the loot, but Harry Speed and Les Hooper would be following along — probably at some distance. They would not be willing to let the money they had awaited for ten years slip away.

Stoker he bound and gagged, dragging him into a clump of brush behind the barn. It would not be a comfortable night for the stumpy gunman, but then it was no time for sympathy. In other circumstances Stoker might not have had a cold night to suffer through, or a dawn approaching to warm him again.

Laredo might have been forced to shoot the man dead.

10

Asa Taylor looked up from the rickety kitchen table where he was picking over the remains of a previously roasted chicken by candlelight. The outlaw leader's pistol, Laredo noticed, was on the table at his elbow.

'Want something to eat?' Asa asked, although it was obvious there wasn't much meat left on the bird's carcass.

'No, I think I'll turn in. My shoulder's hurting me quite a bit.'

'You can see a doctor tomorrow in Bisbee after we've finished our business.'

'Yes, that's been on my mind. That and finding a few boys to help me with the herd.' Laredo asked, 'I don't suppose any of your men would like to stay around for a few days and help out? I'll pay them well.'

'I think they've all got their minds set

on being somewhere else,' Asa Taylor said, managing not to break a smile.

'I see,' Laredo said, trying to look like a man disappointed. 'Well,' he said, lifting a hand, 'I'll see you in the morning, then.'

'Early,' Asa Taylor answered. 'It's going to be a busy day.'

It might prove to be a busier day than even Asa could imagine, Laredo thought as he tramped the short distance to his room. On his bed with its thin mattress, the faint glow of the coming moon shining through the narrow window, Laredo wondered exactly what he could do now. He didn't want to waste a lot of time examining the horse herd, but then, 'Larry Cotton' would. He figured he would let Asa make the call on that one. The man would not wish to spend much time looking at horses either; he was bound for Colorado, and his gang would be eager to travel. Possibly Asa would just curtail things by offering the ponies at an extraordinary bargain price, one Cotton could not turn away from, so that they could reach Bisbee and the bank early.

But it was one thing to make plans and often quite another for them to work out the way they had been envisioned, as Laredo well knew. He slept fitfully, knowing that the outlaws might change their minds about him. His shoulder ached and flared with fiery pain. He also worried about how he was going to take the cautious Asa Taylor in Bisbee, knowing that the man would be wary. Then there was the chance that Stoker would somehow free himself from his bonds and return to the house, signaling the end of Laredo's charade.

Despite these thoughts and the pain, Laredo managed to sleep a little off and on until the first gray light began to seep into the room, announcing the arrival of sunrise. It was the day he had been looking forward to, one he was loath to face.

Stoker still lay bound and gagged where he was, apparently, for they had not come for him even though Les

Hooper would have returned as well overnight. Perhaps he had gone directly to bed, unconcerned with the where-abouts of his long-time gang associate. That was likely; as Laredo knew each man had his mind set only on the money. To find a man missing, even if he had been a friend, would not worry them greatly. It would only make the others' slice of the pie larger.

Once they had visited the money trader in Colorado, they would not be riding out together. Each man would be wary of the other's greed. Safety would require each playing a lone hand.

Asa was at the kitchen table with Harry Speed. Asa wore a fixed smile. Harry Speed had his constantly glower-ing dark eyes on Laredo. The presence of these two alone seemed to indicate that Les Hooper had returned to the lookout post. The odds for Laredo were still not good; he stuck with the original plan.

The house was chill in the gray morning. The wink of a golden ray of sunrise shafted into the house through the kitchen window, and Asa rose, sparing a single glance — a warning? — for Harry Speed.

'Good, you're ready to begin, then,' he said to Laredo. As an afterthought, he asked as if he cared, 'How's the shoulder?'

'It'll hang together until I can see a doctor,' Laredo replied, not meeting Speed's gaze.

'Good. Let's take a little tour, then,' Asa Taylor said, picking up his rifle.

They walked to the river, for which Laredo was grateful. He still wasn't sure he could saddle his gray with one arm. The horses, apparently used to being fed at this time of the morning, gathered around them as they reached the river-bank.

'They like me,' Asa Taylor said in an uncharacteristic voice, and it was obvious to Laredo that Taylor cared for his horses. If he had remained as Randall Nye, trading and selling, he might have had a life he enjoyed. But he had made his choice: perhaps the years of waiting had only intensified his desire to see things through to the end.

'Now, that's a horse,' Laredo commented, as Taylor stroked the muzzle of a chestnut gelding, its coat burnished by the low light of the rising sun.

Laredo took his time, making a show of examining teeth and hocks, counting heads. After a while Asa grew impatient. His eyes kept going to the house where Harry Speed waited within reach of the stolen money.

'Well,' Asa snapped, 'are we going to do business or not?'

'Yes, we are,' Laredo answered. 'I'm just trying to figure out which ponies I can afford with the money I have.'

'What have you got in all?' Asa asked sharply.

Laredo invented a number which seemed neither too small nor too large — certainly less than the herd was worth. Asa Taylor didn't hesitate. He said, 'They're yours, all of them. Take them!'

He walked back toward the house, a man disappointed. Not with the price which both knew was very low, but with himself, possibly over the loss of the house and the horse herd which had meant so much to him. Laredo felt a twinge of pity, but then a man makes his own choices, does he not?

'Saddle up,' Asa growled. 'I want to get to the bank early and be gone from here by day's end.'

'I might need some help saddling my horse,' Laredo said apologetically.

'You got it done last night, didn't you?' Asa Taylor asked, his flat face a mask, his expression unreadable.

'Taking it down is one thing. Putting it back up is another,' Laredo said, trying for his amiable Larry Cotton grin.

'All right,' Asa agreed, as Laredo had known he would. 'I'll have Harry come out and give you a hand. I want to get our business completed today.'

No more than Laredo did, but he was far from optimistic about his chances. He walked to the tumbledown barn, squinting into the rising sun. There was a brief urge to go to where Stoker lay, to check up on the outlaw, but he did not dare do so. Instead he waited in the dark, musty interior of the barn, smoothing his blanket on the horse's back, slipping its bit, fastening the throat latch of the bridle.

He half-expected Harry Speed to confront him, to say he wished he had killed him with his bullet, that he did not trust him, to question him about Stoker, but Speed did none of these. He simply strode in, spat once on the ground, grabbed Laredo's saddle and threw it over the gray's back. It seemed that Harry Speed had adjusted to circumstances and only wanted Asa to complete his dealings so that they could get on with their main business in Colorado.

Within the hour Asa Taylor and Laredo were riding the trail back to Bisbee. Asa continually looked back. Laredo didn't have to wonder why. Asa was carrying all of the Red Butte gang's assets in his saddle-bags which he had thrown over the haunches of his big black horse. These bags were full, but not weighty. They held the $10,000 cash money Roger Franklin had stolen from his bank at Flagstaff in a vain attempt to placate his outlaw friends and the $50,000 in gold certificates taken in the Mountain Springs robbery. There was no way in the world Harry Speed would let that money just drift out of his life. Also Les Hooper was still around somewhere, probably standing watch on one of the low ridges that lined the road.

As far as Asa knew, Stoker remained on the ranch as well. Stoker would want to ride with Speed to make sure that Asa had nothing dirty planned. For all Laredo knew Stoker was still in the game. It was possible the little bully boy had freed himself, or that Speed had found him. Asa Taylor might be considering duplicitous maneuvers, but he knew he was running the risk of enraging three armed and experienced men if he actually tried anything. Laredo did not think the gang leader would do that. He was keeping the loot with him for his own security. He would share, if reluctantly, when the time came.

Except if Laredo had his way there would be nothing to share, for he meant to reclaim the bank money one way or another once they reached Bisbee.

Laredo began to talk to the jittery Asa Taylor along the trail. As Larry Cotton might, he began discussing the attributes of the horses, the big chestnut and the two strapping yearling colts Taylor owned. Asa listened and made amiable responses at first, then he began to show irritation; his mind obviously wasn't on his horses except as merchandise to be disposed of. Taylor was nervous as a cat by the time they reached Bisbee. He must have been thinking about everything that could go wrong — as was Laredo.

They reached the bank and tied up

their horses shortly before it was time for the bank to open. Laredo glanced toward the sheriff's office and then looked at the Blue Belle restaurant. Had Alicia gone back to work at the place? If she saw the two of them in town together, what sort of interpretation would she place on it?

There was no time to ponder further. Walking up the street toward them now was the banker himself, a stout man named Henning, who glanced at his gold pocket watch as he approached. The banker put on his businessman's smile as he stepped up onto the plankwalk and fished his keys out of his pocket.

'Good morning, Mr Nye!' he said cheerfully. 'Hello, Laredo. Back so soon?'

Asa Taylor stiffened and his own smile became a scowl. There was no reason for Taylor to know his face, but Laredo had been on his job for a long time now, and his name must have been mentioned now and then around outlaw campfires.

Asa Taylor made to back away, but Laredo didn't give him the chance. He grabbed the man by his leather vest, clamped down hard on Asa's other hand which was pawing at his pistol, and back-heeled the man, sending Asa Taylor roughly to a seat on the plankwalk, his pistol clattering free. From up the street Glen Radcliffe came rushing toward them, his silver star glinting in the sunlight.

'What's going on here?' Radcliffe panted as he approached, gun drawn. The banker shrugged his ignorance and stepped back.

'I brought Asa Taylor to visit you,' Laredo said. 'There's an almighty load of evidence in his saddlebags.'

'So Nye was Taylor,' the sheriff said.

'He was . . . is,' Laredo replied.

Radcliffe helped Asa to his feet. For a moment Asa struggled as if he would try to escape, but Radcliffe's grip was firm and Laredo was watching, his hand on his holstered Colt. Asa gave it up. They walked toward the sheriff's office, Radcliffe guarding his prisoner, Laredo leading his gray horse and Asa Taylor's black.

'Things are getting busy around here,' Radcliffe said. 'I had a wanted man come in just yesterday and give himself up only an hour before I got a poster on him delivered on the afternoon stage.'

'Roger Franklin,' Laredo said and the sheriff lifted his eyebrows and pursed his lips.

'How'd you know about that?'

'I sent him in,' Laredo said.

'You're keeping my jail full,' Radcliffe said. 'Any more coming?' He nudged Asa toward the jail door. Earl, the sheriff's deputy, was watching, pistol in one hand, a sausage sandwich in the other.

Laredo didn't answer then. He slipped Asa's saddle-bags from his horse and followed Radcliffe into the office. Earl was already hustling a fuming, cursing Asa Taylor down the hall to a cell. Laredo's mind was on Radcliffe's question. Would there be more coming? Of course there would. The entire Red Butte gang — what was left of them — would have to follow Asa and the money into Bisbee.

'How's the bank on shipping money?' Laredo asked, as he settled into a chair after first removing Roger Franklin's black coat. Radcliffe looked at the bloody shirt Laredo wore underneath, but he said nothing about that, answering the question first.

'Stuart Henning's bank has a good reputation. Why do you ask? Laredo, let me get you a doctor.'

'I'd be obliged,' Laredo admitted. His body was weakening with every hour the gunshot wound went untreated, and it was still leaking fresh blood. When Earl returned, jingling his keys, Radcliffe dispatched his deputy for a doctor.

Laredo took Asa Taylor's saddle-bags to the sheriff's desk and dumped the contents on it. Sheaves of greenbacks with the Bank of Flagstaff bands still on them tumbled out. From the other bag, Laredo produced a stack of ornately decorated gold certificates. Series B.

He checked the serial numbers although there was no real need to do so. One bill was missing, breaking the sequence — the $500 certificate Asa Taylor had tried to cash at the bank, claiming that he had gotten it in a horse trade with some unknown man. This was probably now tucked in his boot, or hidden at the Nye ranch somewhere.

'I asked about the bank because I don't want to be riding north carrying all of this,' Laredo said, seating himself again, holding his arm tightly. 'As to your question about whether there would be any more prisoners coming' — he nodded at the money — 'I think you can be pretty sure there will be.'

Radcliffe nodded and tugged at the ends of his wildly flourishing mustache. 'The Red Butte boys, you mean.'

'That's who I mean,' Laredo confirmed. 'Have you interviewed Roger Franklin yet?'

'Just enough to hear his confession, which he offered without being asked. Why? Do you think he has more he can tell me?'

'Probably not much, but he can link these two crimes together and tell you the names of the men he dealt with.'

Radcliffe nodded. 'That would be enough to get new warrants signed for those boys — I told you the old ones had expired.'

'I'd talk to the judge as soon as possible. I don't think the Red Butte boys will delay long.'

'No, I don't either. I can't have them storming my jail trying to break Asa Taylor out or trying to crack the bank. I'm going to have to call in all my deputies for some extra duty.

'Laredo, you sure have turned Bisbee upside down. Next time you come around, leave me out of it.'

Radcliffe was almost smiling when he

said that, but not quite. Laredo couldn't blame the man. He had been put in an uncomfortable situation. His peaceful little routine was no more — not until the entire Red Butte gang had been eliminated.

And Laredo was not going to be able to offer any help. Before Radcliffe's last word had been spoken, the sheriff glanced up and noticed that Laredo had passed out in his chair. The big man was out of any fight.

11

Laredo's eyes opened slowly. He was in a bed somewhere, but where? He tried to stretch his arms but could not. His left shoulder and arm were bound up very tightly with new bandages. He was not alone in the room. As his vision cleared he could see the narrow blonde girl in a pink dress sitting in the corner of the room, working on some needle-point.

She had seen his movements and now she put her sewing aside and came to the bed.

'Hello, Mabel,' he said with a thick tongue.

'You remember my name. Very flattering,' she said. Pouring Laredo a glass of water, she helped him drink.

'Doc said you'd be feeling a little slow. That's the morphine he plugged you with. Says you are absolutely not to try to get up — you'd probably fall on your face.'

'Is that all he said?' Laredo asked, trying his arm again. At least it was all still there, he found.

'Said you were really a stupid man for waiting so long to have it seen to,' Mabel told him with a faint smile.

'There was something I had to do,' Laredo murmured. His eyes were nearly closed again. His eyelids were very heavy.

'I know,' Mabel said, rising to part the flimsy curtains and look out. 'Glen told me a little about it and then he sent me over here to watch you.'

'What about the Blue Belle?'

'Today's my day off,' Mabel said. 'I didn't mind doing Glen a favor.' No, she wouldn't. From what Laredo had seen, the girl definitely had her cap set for Sheriff Radcliffe, and it seemed he had begun to take notice.

'I don't mind at all,' she said again, letting the sheer curtains drop. 'Except in a sort of evil way, I wish . . . ' and then she fell silent. Laredo could guess the rest of what she had been about to say. She wished that it was Radcliffe lying in that bed, needing her attentions.

And it might be soon. Laredo didn't know how many deputies Radcliffe could muster, but it was the sheriff's job to lead them and he would be the first under the guns of the Red Butte boys.

'Stu Henning sent a message to you — do you know him?' Mabel asked.

Laredo answered with a weary nod. 'The banker, yes I do.'

'He said that he is getting transport to Flagstaff immediately. He is hiring a special coach with a shotgun rider. That will be Abel Barnett: he is a mean man, but an honest one . . . ' Mabel caught herself drifting from the point and finished up, 'He said he thought it best to get the money out of town immediately.'

'Good,' Laredo muttered. That was quick work on Henning's part, but then he was in the banking business and knew he might have need of the services of Laredo or someone like him one day. He would want to stay cozy with the Bank Examiner's Office.

'What's Glen Radcliffe up to?' he asked.

There was a hitch in Mabel's voice when she answered, 'Glen has called in all the deputies he could find. They have men out watching the trails into town. Earl and two other men are going to be barricaded inside the jail to prevent an attempt at escape.

'Laredo,' she asked the man with the closed eyes and the bandaged body, 'how many of these Red Butte boys are there?'

'There should be only three,' he told her. Unless they had recruited some help, which seemed unlikely, loath as they were to share any money. That seemed to reassure Mabel.

'Three men?' she said. 'Why, Glen takes care of more men than that by himself every night.'

Laredo did not answer. If he had, it

would have been, 'Not men like these, he hasn't.'

He lay half-sleeping in the room, a cool breeze fluttering around him, trying to think things out. The game was won, but the Red Butte boys would not surrender to the facts — not after ten years of waiting. Three men, he had told Mabel, but were there even that many? He had no way of knowing if Stoker had been found and freed. Probably so. And probably the three men — Harry Speed, Stoker and Les Hooper — had already been in town, following in his and Taylor's tracks, before the sheriff had even begun his preparations.

Their goals now would be to find out from Asa where the money had gotten to — if they could somehow reach the bandit leader — and to recover it. They might know nothing of banker Stuart Henning's plan to ship the gold certificates and stolen greenbacks to Flagstaff, but if the Red Butte gang were in town, they would certainly be watching the bank, and certainly notice a special stagecoach drawing up. There was no need for them to concern themselves with Asa Taylor: they would go directly toward the coach.

Laredo was suddenly wide awake, alert. He could not lose those gold certificates a second time! He struggled to sit up, his muscles lethargic, the pain still present in his shoulder.

'What are you doing?' Mabel asked, coming to the bed again, to push him back with hands to his chest. 'I told you the doctor said — '

'I have to get up,' Laredo said, surprised at his weakness, the ease with which Mabel had pushed him back on the mattress. 'I know what's going to happen; I have to talk to Glen.'

'I'll ask one of the hotel staff to go try to find him.'

'Go yourself — now, it's important,' Laredo said.

'They told me to keep watch over you,' she said, fearful of getting in Glen Radcliffe's bad graces, perhaps.

Bad graces or bad *gracias?*

The thought suddenly occurred to Laredo. Where could the outlaws go to get information concerning what was happening in Bisbee? Who might have overheard private conversations as she served food, virtually invisible to everyone? Who had close ties to the outlaw gang and a large stake in the recovery of the loot?

'Is Alicia working at the Blue Belle?' Laredo asked. Mabel's expression relayed her thoughts that Laredo had gone mad under the influence of the morphine, or was obsessed with trivialities.

'Yes, of course,' she said slowly, like a patient nurse.

Alicia, who was close to Harry Speed and was Les Hooper's wife; Alicia, who wanted her own share of the stolen gold certificates. To whom else would the gang go for information about the events in Bisbee?

Laredo had to get up. He was determined now. He smiled weakly at the hesitant little waitress, feeling bad as he tried to utilize her. 'Please,' he said in a weak voice, 'bring Glen Radcliffe to talk to me.' Then he gave an audible sigh and lay staring at the ceiling, absolutely motionless.

Mabel hesitated, uncertain, then grabbed her knitted shawl, placed it across her shoulders, and crossed the room toward the door. When Laredo heard her boots clicking down the hallway he made the great effort to swing his legs to the floor and begin dressing.

He didn't fall on his face as the doctor had warned, but once as he fumbled and clumsily tried to dress himself, it was only because the room was small, the walls close enough for him to throw up his arm and brace himself before biting floorboard. It was bad enough having only one usable arm, but the swirling fog in his brain, caused he supposed by morphine, fuddled his thoughts enough so that once he caught himself trying to tug up his jeans only to belatedly realize that it was his shirt he had on his foot.

And this was the man who was going out to try to stop the Red Butte gang?

He knew his decision was irrational, that he should take the advice of the doctor and Mabel and simply return to his bed and let Glen Radcliffe handle the badmen. But Laredo was not built that way: he was a bulldog, and slightly fanatical about his work. He would not let these men beat him.

It took Laredo a full half-minute to remember how to open the door to his room and go out. Placing his hat on his head, he started out, stumbling and lurching his way along the hallway. His mind began to clear as he limped forward and slipped out of the hotel by way of the wooden outside staircase. He thought he knew what must be done — if his body would co-operate. His first thought had been to locate Alicia and find out what she knew, but the Blue Belle was in the opposite direction from the bank. It did not matter so much what she knew as making sure that the bank was not robbed again.

Rather, the hired stagecoach, for that would be their target. It would be rough and bloody work, but the Red Butte boys had no back-down in them, and what was one more stagecoach job to this band of outlaws after their string of violent crimes?

Exiting the dusty alley onto the main street of Bisbee which was lying in silent languor on this heated day under a high siesta sun, Laredo had a surprise. His gray horse was standing at the rail of the hotel, saddle and bridle in place. While silently cursing whoever had left the animal there, he also blessed this unknown person. The horse, he was sure, could walk straighter than he could just then.

The horse seemed to swim away in his vision as he approached it, but Laredo grabbed the saddlehorn, determined not to let the animal go. Loosing the gray from the hitch rail, he positioned himself for the dubious proposition of swinging himself aboard. Perspiration rained into Laredo's eyes although he had been out in the sun for only a few minutes. Damn that morphine. The next time, if he had the chance, he would beg the surgeons to just go at it without anesthetics.

If there was a next time.

In his very confused state he thought of Dusty, his red-haired wife, of his home in Crater, of Jake Royle's disappointment when Laredo told his boss he had had enough of tracking men for a living . . . if he could ever make it back that far.

Just now he returned to the immediate problem of how to get aboard his horse and stay there. He was going to get no assistance from his battered and bandaged left arm. Planting his left foot firmly in the stirrup, he gripped the pommel as tightly as he could and swung up with all of his remaining strength. It proved to be more strength than he had thought he had in reserve, for he nearly tumbled over the far side of the horse.

Straightening, breathing hard through his mouth, Laredo let the dry breeze whip the perspiration from him. He still was not thinking straight, and he knew it. Where to go first? Glen Radcliffe's office? No, Radcliffe would probably chase him off to bed at first sight.

He had wanted to talk to Alicia, but that would just be an unnecessary detour if the Red Butte boys had tumbled to the fact that a stagecoach was carrying the $50,000 from Bisbee today. And it was assuming she was even willing to tell Laredo the truth, which seemed unlikely. She had too much invested in the recovery of the gold certificates herself.

All right, then. He would first swing by the bank and warn Stuart Henning that the stage carrying the stolen money would almost certainly be attacked along the line to Flagstaff and that if he had only one shotgun rider — this Abel Barnett — he might consider hiring another trustworthy local man to ride along, perhaps inside the coach itself.

Not that the Red Butte boys would be daunted. They had long experience in defeating this sort of planning by Wells Fargo, Overland and other coach companies as well as independent bank shipments. If only Laredo were ready to ride . . . he wasn't sure right now that he could even make it to the bank. He thought of having Henning send somebody to summon Radcliffe. The trouble was the sheriff believed he already had matters in hand, and would not be willing to leave his jail to respond to a dubious warning.

Laredo knew that the deputies watching the trails to town were waiting for men who had already arrived. And, he had not seen a single man wearing a star on the streets of Bisbee. Mabel had said that Radcliffe was forted up in his jail, believing that the other Red Butte boys would try to bust Asa Taylor out. Laredo wasn't so sure. Harry Speed and the others might have a certain sort of loyalty toward Asa, but it would not be strong enough to send them to try to free him from jail when they had the chance to finally get their hands on the $50,000 and now knew the name of a man in Denver they could deal with to exchange the gold certificates for actual spending money, thanks to Roger Franklin.

Arriving at the bank, Laredo saw no unusual movement, but then the stage would have been pulled up behind the bank, in the alley. At least that was the way Laredo would have handled it.

He had to talk to Henning. Was there any way to do it without having to swing down from the saddle again? He had felt better all in all before Glen had called for a doctor, but then again he would have missed that arm in days to come if Radcliffe had not done so.

Someone walked out of the bank, a farmer by his looks, counting some silver money before dropping it into his leather purse.

'Say, partner,' Laredo called out, 'I'll

give you a silver dollar for telling Mr Henning that I'm out here waiting to see him.'

The farmer glanced at the gaunt man with the injured arm, not liking his looks, and went off without saying a word. The man obviously didn't want to be mixed up in anything. Maybe the word had gotten around town that something was up, and to be careful of strangers. Laredo tried to mutter a curse, found that he hadn't the strength to do so.

He was now concerned that if he got down from his horse he would never get back up again. He thought again of Alicia and the Blue Belle, but doubted he would have much luck there. He could sit there hollering for Henning, looking like a fool, but he had no firm information to give the bank owner regarding a stick-up.

After a few minutes of reeling in the saddle, the world whirling crazily around him while he clung to the saddlehorn, Laredo decided to make his own patrol of the area. If any of the Red Butte boys were lingering in town, he meant to find them. It was improbable that any were here, he considered. They had likely made their own earlier observations and were now looking for a good ambush spot along the well-known road to Flagstaff.

And what could Laredo do about that? Ride after them hard and fast, guns blazing? Not in his present condition. Only one answer to the problem suggested itself: he had intended to return to Flagstaff when his assignment was completed; the gold certificates were heading for Flagstaff in the stagecoach; he was incapable of riding hard and long.

Laredo was going to take himself a little stagecoach ride.

12

Stuart Henning did finally emerge from the bank, looking cautiously up and down the main street as he did so. He goggled a bit as he saw the dusty, bandaged man sitting a horse in front of the bank. Henning thought at first that this one must have been looking for either the doctor or the sheriff, and started to give directions. Then he recognized Laredo through the tape, the dust and the blood.

'Good God! What happened to you? Where are you going, Laredo?'

'To Flagstaff if you'll let me go along,' the man reeling in the saddle answered in a strangled voice. 'In the stagecoach.'

'You're in no fit shape for such an expedition,' Henning objected automatically, approaching Laredo's gray horse.

'Of course I'm not,' Laredo answered

with what he hoped was a smile. 'But, Henning, try to understand me: there's a very good chance that the Red Butte boys are going to come after the gold certificates again. I can't give them up! That is my money.' He stopped, panting, and explained his words. 'I was sent to recover those bonds; I did so. I've put some sweat and some of my blood into securing them. This may be my last job and I won't go out as a failure. My reputation, such as it is, is riding with that money.'

'That doesn't mean that you can make the long trip or that you'd be of any help if the stage were stopped along the road,' Henning said in a way that was almost pitying.

'No, but I'd be of more help than if no one was along.'

Henning seemed to doubt that, also he was wondering where Laredo had gotten his information — Sheriff Radcliffe seemed convinced that the Red Butte boys could be stopped before they even reached town. Nevertheless, the banker was convinced that there was nothing he could do to dissuade the ragged, bloody horseman in front of him that he was wrong. Perhaps he was not.

'I'll find you a seat in the coach and have one of my boys take your horse to the stable, unless — '

'No, I won't want him along, put the old gray up; he's been following a rough trail too,' Laredo replied. 'I'll send for him later. For now, Henning,' he said, 'I'd be obliged if you could find someone to help me clamber down from this saddle before I fall.'

Henning, his mind made up now, signaled to one of his clerks who had been listening in the bank's doorway. The clerk was slight and apparently concerned with his appearance, but he came forward at his boss's beckoning and Laredo slid himself from the saddle. It was a good thing he had asked for help: he landed on his feet, but with his knees buckling uncertainly, his head spinning. He waited a moment, breathing in deeply, bent over at the waist, then grabbed his Winchester from the saddle scabbard and nodded.

'Let's get going.'

Walking around the bank, not through it, Laredo was guided to the stage, which sat in the partially shaded, dry alley. He thought the morphine was wearing off some which made the walking in a straight line easier, but left his shoulder suffering worse pain.

Oh, well, it was the price he would have to pay.

Laredo was introduced to the driver, a whip-thin nervous man named Wilburn Titus wearing fringed gauntlets and a high-riding .38 pistol. Leaning against the wall in the shade was the shotgun rider, Abel Barnett. This one was a different story.

Mabel had described Barnett as a mean man but an honest one. There was no telling what she had meant, but the dark-eyed man with the double-twelve shotgun in his hands looked tough if nothing else. And, in his business, a man had to be tough. There was no telling if Barnett was mean, no way of gauging the man's honesty, but Henning had hired him on and the bank owner was bound to know Barnett better than Laredo did, and obviously trusted him.

'One passenger,' Stuart Henning said, and Barnett seemed to stiffen a little, but he said nothing.

'When are we starting?' Titus, the driver, asked nervously. He had the appearance of a skilled driver, but likely this was the first time he had made a run with $50,000 as his only cargo. It didn't take a genius to realize that it was an invitation to highwaymen — if they knew anything about it. Laredo smiled a little as he stepped into the stage, assisted by the clerk's hand on one elbow.

The bit of amusement was caused by his knowledge that if they were hit by other would-be raiders, the robbers would find themselves wealthy men — on paper — but doomed to follow the route the Red Butte boys had taken, hands filled with useless currency.

No, only the Red Butte boys had a use for the gold certificates, the knowledge of how to exchange the Series B paper. It was only them Laredo had to worry about.

'Does the old man need some cushions?' Barnett asked the banker, referring to Laredo who had seated himself stiffly inside the coach. 'If not, get that strongbox out here and let's get going. I mean to have my supper in Flagstaff.' The man's voice had lowered to an impatient growl.

'I'm sending my men for it right now,' Stuart Henning told Barnett. He walked toward the bank. Pausing, as he passed the coach, he looked in and told Laredo, 'This is going to be hell for you, I imagine, but, funny thing is, I'm glad you're going along. It gives me a little more confidence.'

'We'll get through,' Laredo promised. 'You can wire Flagstaff and tell them we're *en route*.'

Laredo actually felt his confidence

returning as the morphine fog slowly lifted from his brain and the savage pain returned, building in his arm, skull and damaged ribs. They would make it through because they had to. Laredo expected no less of himself.

A small iron box of shoebox size with little apparent weight was lifted into the coach and placed on the floor beside Laredo's boots. Henning hovered nervously in the background as it was strapped down to two iron rings set in the floor. Henning yelled some instructions to the driver and shotgun rider, neither of whom replied, probably believing that no banker had a helpful thing to tell them about their own business.

Henning stepped back inside the rear door of the bank, mopping at his forehead with his handkerchief. Laredo heard the crack of the coachman's whip, felt the coach lurch under him and then they were on their way, rolling out of Bisbee in a storm of yellow dust toward Flagstaff and the mountain country far away.

The road for the present was long and straight, traversing mostly open grasslands. Laredo had checked the action of his Winchester and now sat staring out the window of the stage, trying to calculate how far the Red Butte boys could have traveled since he had seen them last. Not far, he thought, and they would not wish to travel far and wear down their horses which would be needed for their escape. What they would have wanted, with only the three of them to make their assault, would be a place of concealment. Laredo rubbed his forehead with the heel of his hand as he scanned the nearly flat land over which they were passing. With his mind still in a bit of a fog, he might have been making the wrong assumptions.

What the Red Butte boys needed was a sheltered position from which to launch their attack. These were plentiful in the uplands, in wooded country. Laredo had thought that the outlaws would not wish to ride that far north to spring their ambush, but why not? North was the direction they were traveling anyway, to find the money trader in Denver.

Maybe they had it in mind to hit the coach when it inevitably slowed on the mountain grade, when the big pines would conceal them. The stagecoach team would be wearying by then; the driver and shotgun rider would be thinking that they were nearly home free. Laredo now believed that the attack would come later rather than sooner, but he had been wrong before, and he did not relax his vigilance as the stagecoach rolled on across the flats, towing its rooster-tail of dust.

Laredo looked once again at the small strongbox, nudged it with his foot and thought how much of his life now depended on this small iron container — success, failure, life, death, all riding in an inconsequential green-painted coffer.

The hours dragged by. The men in

the box had not exchanged a single word that Laredo had heard. Each seemed silently determined to successfully complete his job. There was none of that shouted banter between driver and guard one usually heard aboard an ordinary coach.

Laredo was bone-weary; if not for the pain keeping him awake, he might have dozed off despite the urgency of the situation.

He smelled them before he had seen them. Leaning his head out the window of the coach, he could make out the rising, pine-clotted hills ahead of them. They were on a road he knew well, heading to a place he knew well. Beyond the forest-clad hills lay Flagstaff. Not much longer than an hour's travel would find them among the trees, winding their way upward.

Laredo leaned back in the seat, wondering, hoping he had been wrong about the intentions of Harry Speed, Les Hooper and Stoker. It seemed they could not have had the time to come this far on tired horses. Still, as the stage slowed and began the slow, twisting ascent, Laredo's attention was intense. The four-horse team labored a little on the grade, but these were in superb condition and well trained. Laredo heard Wilburn Titus use his long-handled whip only once as they climbed through the pines and occasional cedar trees; the shade beneath them was blue-black in this light as the trees in close ranks blocked out the sun.

There was nothing to be seen out the windows, only the swaying of the trees and the occasional sight of a couple of woodland wilderness squirrels bounding from limb to limb.

And then Laredo saw something, or thought he did. A shadow rushing from shade to shade not far off the trail, screened by the big pines. He started to bang on the roof of the stage, but was not sure enough to do so. Fifteen seconds later, it was already too late for warnings.

The close flash of a rifle muzzle

showed through the timber and there was the heavy thud of a bullet meeting flesh. Abel Barnett let loose a roaring curse followed by two closely spaced shotgun blasts from the wagon box. An unseen man howled with pain in the woods. Then the horses were running, driverless, and Laredo knew that it must have been Wilburn Titus who had caught lead. The horses plunged on through the deep forest, and without a pair of guiding hands to restrain them, they took the easiest path open to them. Lining out on a low valley, well off the Flagstaff trail, the coach raced on with Barnett presumably trying to grab the reins and reload his shotgun at the same time.

Even in prime condition, Laredo would have found clambering up the side of the coach, swinging into the box, daunting. Just now he knew it was impossible. He could only wait as the horses thundered on. He tried his best to look back, knowing that the Red Butte boys would never give it up. He was jounced around like a rag doll inside the coach. Grasping for a firm handhold, he found none.

Barnett must have at least partially recovered the reins, for he felt the team slowing, turning slightly upland. And behind them now, Laredo spotted pursuers. He could not be sure, but it looked like Harry Speed and Les Hooper. Both wore bandannas as masks. Both had rifles in their hands. That meant that the man Barnett had hit with his shotgun blast was Stoker, who had been better off before he rejoined the gang. But then, neither was Stoker going to quit while his cut of $50,000 was at stake. Those cuts were now getting rapidly larger: Speed and the redheaded husband of Alicia were each set to win a $25,000 share.

If they could catch up, and it looked like they could. Their horses may have been tired, but still a single mounted man was quicker than any coach.

'Can you slow them anymore?' Laredo shouted up toward the box. 'I'm jolting around too much to take decent aim!'

The answer took a moment in coming. 'You still back there, then?'

'I'm here!'

'Hold on, then,' Barnett shouted down. 'I'm going to try to turn them uphill though I've only got half the ribbons. It'll slow them, and when we come around you should have a good shot out the left window.'

With little hesitation then, Abel Barnett managed to turn the team uphill across the meadow. The rear end of the stagecoach canted up and then settled with a heavy thud, jolting Laredo across its width. The stage horses were now gradually slowing, winded and running uphill. Laredo dragged himself to the left-hand window. The outlaws were much nearer than he had thought. He settled the front bead sight of his Winchester on the galloping Harry Speed's chest — the man he took for the most dangerous — fired, missed, cursed, levered in a new cartridge. His second bullet did not miss. It sent Harry Speed flying from his horse to sprawl against the grass. Laredo could not tell if he had killed the man or not, though he thought so.

Les Hooper drew up his horse, or at least let it slow. The youngest of the gang, the one Laredo had been told wished to be as tough as Asa Taylor and as good with a gun as Harry Speed but didn't have it in him, seemed to have given it up.

Now as Laredo watched with disbelief following a moment's panic, a band of armed men emerged from the woods to the north. At first he wondered if he had miscalculated again: there had been more men in the Red Butte gang than he knew about to account for. Then, even at a distance, he recognized the pudgy man who rode in their lead on a lively-looking red roan. It was hard to mistake Jake Royle even at a distance. Beside him were four men from the enforcement arm; Laredo knew two of them personally.

'Friends of yours?' Abel Barnett called down from the box of the now-halted stagecoach.

'Yes,' Laredo answered. 'Friends of mine.'

Barnett grunted some sort of response and began gathering all of the reins to the team. Laredo slipped from the coach, stumbled but remained upright and staggered forward.

'Will Titus make it?' he asked a gloomy Barnett.

'He didn't,' the shotgun rider replied. 'Damn shame, too. Titus was all right.'

Laredo stood awaiting the arrival of Jake Royle and his hastily assembled men. They had slowed now, seeing that there was no further need for hurry.

'There he goes!' a man Laredo knew as Ken Barber shouted, lifting a pointing finger. He turned his pony and spurred it, followed by a man whose name Laredo did not know. They were in hot pursuit of Les Hooper, whose pony now showed signs of faltering.

That horse had had a long run on this day.

'They'll get him,' Jake Royle said, remaining in the saddle of his roan. 'You know I don't like loose ends.'

'You don't like riding much anymore either,' Laredo said, 'but here you are — and just in time.'

'Stuart Henning wired us at the office. He said you were *en route*. I wondered why you were aboard the coach — I knew there must have been a reason, like not being sure the job was over yet. I figured we'd better come out and meet you.'

'Glad you did.'

Both men looked to the west as the enforcement agents rode back, prodding a bedraggled-looking Les Hooper before them. Laredo told Jake, 'There's another one, I think, lying dead back along the trail. His name was Stoker.' Laredo told him approximately where the body could be found. Jake sent one of his men back in that direction.

'That seems to be the end of the Red

Butte boys,' Royle said. He swung heavily from his horse. 'Let's see what you've brought back.'

They opened the strongbox with Abel Barnett and Ken Barber looking on. Jake Royle riffled through the ornate gold certificates and nodded. 'Let's get this back to where it belongs,' Jake said, closing the box again. 'And let's get this man to a bed,' he added, nodding at Laredo. He asked Abel Barnett, 'Can you handle the stage team?'

'I can,' Barnett told him.

'Good, that's a skill I never learned,' Jake said. He looked again at Laredo, who was now leaning heavily against the side of the coach. 'Ken,' he instructed Barber, 'maybe you'd better go along inside. Hold Laredo up so he doesn't flop on the floor.'

They did it that way, Ken Barber's horse used for transporting the body of Wilburn Titus in to Flagstaff.

Laredo awoke in a hotel bed he did not remember getting into. A new morning sun was shining beyond his window. He was still tired, dead-tired, but the pain in his shoulder had lessened appreciably. He had to be careful about moving it, but it was better and Laredo decided that he had to get up: he was as hungry as a man could get.

The hallway was empty. The late risers were still asleep and the travelers and businessmen were already up and gone. He moved carefully down the staircase to the hotel lobby. There was no one at the desk either. He found that he could move without those jolts of pain, that his head was clear and not plagued with dizziness. Outside, the new sun was bright, reflecting off the windows of the storefronts. He could smell breakfast cooking nearby. A yellow mongrel bitch trotted past with two pups bounding along after. A kid in a straw hat came chasing after the dogs.

It was a fine day to be alive.

13

After breakfast Laredo stood on the restaurant porch for a few minutes before, with a sigh, he started walking toward Jake Royle's office. He was going to have to make his report sooner or later, and this one was going to be a little long, a little complicated. He passed Ken Barber, who was coming down the stairs to Royle's office. Laredo nodded to him.

'I'm off. New assignment,' Barber said. 'You wouldn't want to hear about it.'

No, he thought, as Barber continued on his way, he wouldn't want to hear about it. He didn't care to hear about any office business for a good long time, if ever again. That was still a lingering thought: did Laredo want to call this his last job? It was a huge temptation to do so.

Pushing open Jake Royle's door he caught a hint of cigar smoke although no cigar was in evidence. The window was open, a light breeze passing through. Jake was in his usual position, behind his desk with his boots off. On this morning he wore a blue silk shirt and had his hair plastered down.

'Expecting the governor?' Laredo asked, lowering himself gingerly into a wooden chair.

'A man can't spruce up a little without hearing remarks,' Jake growled. He smiled then. 'I've been interviewing recruits, Laredo. Someone is going to have to take up the slack for you.

'One of them,' Jake added quietly, 'is a female.'

He waited for Laredo to react, but got no response. 'All right,' Jake said, pulling a yellow tablet from his desk drawer, licking the tip of a pencil, 'tell me all from the moment you left Flagstaff.'

Laredo did, skipping over only a few events which would add nothing to the report. When they had finally finished, Jake had flipped over four pages of his tablet filled with his scribble. Royle frowned at the pad and pushed it aside. He told Laredo, 'I got a wire from Bisbee. Sheriff Radcliffe has hired a man to bring up your gray horse. It should be here by tomorrow morning.

'All right, Laredo,' Royle said, tilting back in his chair, looking hungrily at his desk drawer where Laredo was certain more cigars rested, 'this is the point at which you usually tender your resignation, saying you've had enough.'

'This time I might stick by it,' Laredo said. 'If you could find me a job like yours. I do have a home and a wife, if you'll remember, and I see them just often enough so that I don't forget what they look like.'

'I know, I know,' Jake said, holding up his pudgy hands. 'But I need you, Laredo. After you've had a good long rest you might think different about any such decision. Look at all the work I have here,' he said, thumbing a stack of reports. 'Men who need to be caught — and you're the best. Think of your own reputation.'

'I know, Jake,' Laredo answered with a smile. 'That's one reason I was thinking this is a good time to quit. I mean, having done the impossible, how can I ever top myself?'

Jake didn't get it or didn't think it was funny. Either way, it was time to be going. His gray horse was being delivered, and it was time for Laredo to deliver himself to his little redheaded wife in Crater, Arizona.

He stepped out into the hall, took four steps away and paused. He slowly counted to ten and then caught the sweet-pungent smell of a burning cigar from Jake's office. Grinning, Laredo went on his way.

Crossing the street, he saw a small feminine figure dart from an alley and rush toward the town jail. It couldn't have been . . . but he thought it was and started that way himself. Entering the jail he saw the marshal and a narrow deputy going about their business of arranging the desk and files. Further along he saw a woman visitor in skirts, talking to one of the prisoners. Her voice rose a little and then burst out with:

'And you called *me* stupid!'

At the same moment the woman drew a concealed handgun from her skirt and she touched off, the roar of the gun loud in the confined area of the jail. Hoisting her skirts she turned toward the door, and Laredo stepped aside, hands raised, as Alicia rushed past him and out the open doorway.

The deputy was first to the jail cell. 'It's the new prisoner, Marshal. That Les Hooper. The lady shot him dead!'

The marshal, his face angry, settled his eyes on Laredo. 'You were closest to her; why didn't you grab her?'

'She had a gun,' Laredo answered. 'Besides, it's no concern of mine.'

The marshal was furious, and he rushed out into the street, gun drawn. Laredo was behind him. Looking up and down the street, neither saw a sign of a small dark woman. Grumbling, the marshal pushed past Laredo and went back inside, yelling at his deputy. Laredo continued to stand there for a moment, then walked off back toward his hotel.

They might catch her, but Alicia was a clever woman, and she had likely had a horse saddled and ready behind the buildings. Yes, they might catch her and bring her in for killing her husband, but Laredo had the idea that the woman was now riding south as fast as her horse could carry her and would not be stopped until she was back in Mexico.

In the morning, Laredo would be riding south as well, but not as far as Alicia. He was returning to Crater for the first time in a long while. Dusty was waiting there for him, and the two of them had many, many things to discuss.

We do hope that you have enjoyed reading this large print book.

Did you know that all of our titles are available for purchase?

We publish a wide range of high quality large print books including:
Romances, Mysteries, Classics
General Fiction
Non Fiction and Westerns

Special interest titles available in large print are:
The Little Oxford Dictionary
Music Book, Song Book
Hymn Book, Service Book

Also available from us courtesy of Oxford University Press:
Young Readers' Dictionary
(large print edition)
Young Readers' Thesaurus
(large print edition)

For further information or a free brochure, please contact us at:
Ulverscroft Large Print Books Ltd.,
The Green, Bradgate Road, Anstey,
Leicester, LE7 7FU, England.
Tel: (00 44) **0116 236 4325**
Fax: (00 44) **0116 234 0205**

MCANDREW'S STAND

Bill Cartright

Jenny McAndrew and her two sons live in the valley known as McAndrew's Pass. When they hear that the new Rocky Mountains Railroad Company has plans to lay a line through the valley — and their farm — they are devastated at the prospect of their simple lives being destroyed. Clarence Harper, the ruthless boss of the railroad company, is not a man to brook opposition. But in the McAndrews, he finds one family that will not be bullied into submission . . .